MOCCASIN SQUARE GARDENS

MOCCASIN SQUARE GARDENS

RICHARD VAN CAMP

SHORT STORIES

Douglas & McIntyre

Douglas and McIntyre (2013) Ltd.
P.O. Box 219, Madeira Park, BC, VON 2H0
www.douglas-mcintyre.com

Edited by Barbara Pulling
Copy edited by Cheryl Cohen
Cover design by Anna Comfort O'Keeffe and Richard Van Camp
Cover illustration based on Tessa Macintosh photograph of Dene beadwork on
    moccasin upper, ca. 1987 (artist unknown).
Text design by Carleton Wilson
Printed and bound in Canada
Printed on 100% post-consumer fibres

Canada Council   Conseil des Arts
for the Arts   du Canada

BRITISH COLUMBIA
ARTS COUNCIL
An agency of the Province of British Columbia

Douglas and McIntyre (2013) Ltd. acknowledges the support of the Canada Council for the Arts, which last year invested $153 million to bring the arts to Canadians throughout the country.

Nous remercions le Conseil des arts du Canada de son soutien. L'an dernier, le Conseil a investi 153 millions de dollars pour mettre de l'art dans la vie des Canadiennes et des Canadiens de tout le pays.

We also gratefully acknowledge financial support from the Government of Canada and from the Province of British Columbia through the BC Arts Council and the Book Publishing Tax Credit.

LIBRARY AND ARCHIVES CANADA CATALOGUING IN PUBLICATION

Title: Moccasin Square Gardens : short stories / Richard Van Camp.

Names: Van Camp, Richard, 1971- author.

Identifiers: Canadiana (print) 20190055294 | Canadiana (ebook) 20190055308 |
    ISBN 9781771622165 (softcover) | ISBN 9781771622172 (HTML)

Classification: LCC PS8593.A5376 M63 2019 | DDC C813/.54—dc23

I'm going to dedicate this collection to the Fort Smith "Smoking Tree" across from PWK High School, my old high school. The gossip there was so hot that a lightning strike had to take the tree out before it split the universe in two. Also, to the Fort Smith Christmas Tree, who radiates inside and reaches now in memory to all who witnessed her. And to the memory of the *Slave River Journal*. I miss you so.

As well, I'd like to dedicate this book to the memory of Trevor Evans. Brother of my heart. Called home way too soon.

"First punch has to be real good."
—My mom

Contents

Aliens

I wanna tell you a beautiful story, and I've been waiting for somebody very special to tell it to. I guess it's no secret now: the Star People are here. We can see a ship way up high: its outline. No lights. It's like a big, dark, oblong stone in the sky. Most people just watch TV or Facebook now, waiting for something to happen. Some people call the ships obelisks. Apparently, there's a huge one miles high over every continent, and the oceans are boiling. Gently, though, so no fish are dying. There's a simmering to the water, and scientists are saying that the oceans and rivers are being cleansed. It's like the Star People—that's what our Elders call them—are helping us.

Church bells all over the world chime every hour on the hour now, but I'm not sure why. One of the young men here one night got drunk and took his dad's rifle and shot at the ship. When he woke up he didn't have any hair. It was all there, right on his pillow. He wasn't hurt; he's just…embarrassed.

Some of us—like me—I still go to work. The Star People are here, but the bills don't stop. Plus you gotta get

11

out of the house, right? You gotta check the mail and get groceries, hey?

Many of us left Fort Smith only to return to the NWT years later. We went off to college, or university, or trade schools. Many of us have found relationships, lost relationships, refound love. People have raised their children— some people I went to school with are grandparents now.

And I'm so proud of them. Nothing beats a Christmas concert at JBT Elementary on December 17 every year, right? 'Cause you look around onstage and you see the kids; you feel the pride in the room, that these are our families. We've raised them together. The people I went to school with, they're the teachers of my children, my niece, my nephews right now, and we're all doing great. Everyone's healthy in my family, as far as I know, and I'm so grateful for that.

There's one man who never really left town, and— I'm gonna call him Jimmy for the sake of this story. So Jimmy's family owns the hardware store, and he's always been quiet. He's always been gentle.

My grandfather once cured a relation of Jimmy's. My grandfather was a holy man. His name was Edzazii. No English. A very traditional Tłı̨chǫ Dene man. And they say my grandfather pulled a hummingbird of fire out of a little boy's mouth, from under his tongue. And he showed that little boy this little bird that had been living in his mouth. And he explained this was the reason that little boy couldn't speak like other people. This was why his voice kept locking. And hundreds of people saw this little hummingbird that my grandfather pulled out of this little boy's mouth, and my ehtsèe let that little bird go over Marion Lake. They saw my ehtsèe's power. When that bird of fire left, it flew like a .30-30 shot, and it exploded into sound and sparks. And my grandfather walked all the way back to that little boy, and he said, "Now speak." That little boy started to speak—and they said his knees were just shaking. And that little boy never stuttered again. That was Jimmy's dad. And they say every time he prays, he thanks my grandfather for releasing that little bird from his mouth.

So I guess you can say me and Jimmy are related in the medicine way.

Jimmy's always been in the background of our community. He's always been a mystery. He's always been cruising around by himself. He's always standing, leaning against the back wall at the Christmas concert. Never goes up to dance at any of the gatherings. Never comes into the drum dance, now that the tea dance is back and the drum dance is back. Never participates in hand games. He will go for a burger, but he'll be last in line at Aboriginal Day or Canada Day. He'll wait around for, you know, the second run at the fish fry. He's never been one to go to the front. And I used to wonder about him. I always wondered, like, *Why didn't you leave? Like, weren't you ever curious about the city? When did you decide to live a quiet, gentle life?*

'Cause the worry, from my point of view, was that his was a forgettable life. Because, who knew you? Who did you ever love? Who did you ever—who did you ever give yourself to? I always worried about that with him. I always wondered about that.

Well, little while ago, my niece was in the hardware store looking for lights. 'Member, there was that big rebate: if you switch your house to LED lights, you get, you know, free LED lights, and all that. Some government thing.

And so my niece is in there one day, and Jimmy walks up to her and he says, "Uh, hi," he says. (We'll call my niece Shandra. She's twenty-five now.) "Hi, Shandra," he says. "Can I help you?" and she says, "Oh, I'm looking for these LED lights—the government's giving a rebate?" And he says, "Oh, yeah. They sold out really quick, but we have more in the storage room." And she says, "Oh." He says, "I'll go ... I'll go get 'em for you." She says, "Oh, thanks."

So he come back after a while with the LED lights and he said, "Well, I was wondering what you're doing tonight." And she said, "Oh, uh, I don't know. I'm just taking it easy, I guess." And he said, "Well, I was wondering if I could take you out for supper." And she said, "Oh! Why?" And he said, "Well, I'd like to just—take you out for supper and get to talk with you." And she said, "Oh, like a date?" And he got really shy and he goes, "Well, if you wanna call it that." And so she said, "Oh, well, wow, yeah, what a surprise—okay, sure!" And he goes, "Well, do you want me to pick you up in my truck?" And she said, "Oh, no, I'll just walk there." And he says, "Oh, I'd love to pick you up in my truck." And she says, "Oh, no. It's okay, Jimmy, I'll—I'll just walk there."

'Cause she didn't want the town to see them driving around, right? 'Cause this is serious business, right? My niece knows her way. In a small town, how you arrive to a date is very serious. Also, which part of the restaurant you take your date to. Do you go on the café side, or do you go to the *fancy* side?

So he said, "Uh, okay, ah, so, tonight, six o'clock?" And she said, "Okay, well, I'll meet you there." And he goes, "Well, you know, do you want reservations under my name or yours?" And she said, "Oh! Well, uh, maybe yours, Jimmy," and he said, "Okay," and he goes, "So six o'clock: reservations under my name." And he said, "I want you to know it's on me. Anything that you want. This is really special to me, and I want it to be special for you." And she said, "Are you serious? Like you're talkin' steak and lobster?" And he goes, "Whatever you want." And she said, "Oh, I was just kidding. I would never order steak and lobster." And he goes, "Well, we should. We should order steak and lobster!" She says, "Wow, Jimmy, this is … this is really—sweet. Okay." "Okay, well, I'll see you there," he goes. "Maybe after we could go to the landslide and watch the Star People. At around ten o'clock there's a hum to the ship you can feel in the earth," he says. "Like, if you take off your shoes." And she says, "Oh, well now: we'll see. I should go."

She was really flustered. And he goes, "Well, don't you want your LED lights?" And she said, "Uh, I just, I need to think about this." And he goes, "Well, what's to think about?" And she said, "It's just that, um, a lot of people who ask me out on dates, it's not because they want me. It's because they want my friend Roberta."

And I guess he said, "Roberta? I don't know Roberta. I don't really wanna know her. I mean I'm happy she's your best friend, but," he said, "I'm interested in you." And she said, "Well, you have to excuse me. I'm really surprised, 'cause you never really talked to me before." And he says, "Well, we say hi." And she goes, "Well, yeah, but barely. I don't want to make you feel bad or anything. It's just, I'm nervous. It's been a while since anybody's asked me out." And he said, "Well, I'm really surprised to hear that." And she goes, "Well, it's true." And he goes, "I promise you, I'm not after Roberta," he says. "I'm after you."

That made her pause, I guess. And then she's like, "Well, you know, Jimmy, if we go for a date, this changes everything. You realize that." And he goes, "Well, that's what I'm counting on." "Son of a gun," she said. "Okay, well, I'm gonna go. I want to get a little dressed up for tonight." And he goes, "Well, I'll get dressed up, too." And she says, "Okaaaay. So, see you tonight at six." And he goes, "Well, what are we gonna do about these LED lights?" And she says, "Well, let's see how this date goes." And he says, "Oh! Okay—well, they'll be waitin' here for you." And she says, "Well, never mind that. I gotta go home and get ready."

Right, so, what she did was she went home, and she started calling around to all of us aunties, and she asked us, "What do you know about Jimmy? Like, why is he alone? Why's he been alone?"

Nobody could come up with anything. And she said, "Listen, don't tell anybody, but I'm going on a date with him." And we're like "Gasp! Oh my God! As soon as it's over you have to call!" Right? "Let us know what he's like, whether it's tomorrow morning or at seven thirty tonight when you come home." This was better than *The Young and the Restless*! She said, "Okay, okay, but don't tell any-body!" And we said, "To our graves. To our graves!" Top secret, but we were on speakerphone crossing our fingers, hey? Yep.

So, she got a little gussied up, and she went to the Pelican, and sure enough Jimmy was there. And he was dressed up: nice long-sleeved shirt that he'd ironed, slacks and a thin black belt. He even wore suit shoes, she told us later.

She'd never seen him like this before. Nobody had. He was a new man. And they ordered. He insisted that they order the steak and lobster, I guess. And they had gin-ger ale mixed with cranberry juice—Indian champagne, we call it. Yep. They had a really beautiful supper. And at some point she said to Jimmy, "Well, now that I've got you all to myself, like, I wanna ask you something." And he said, "Anything you want." So she said, "You've always lived, like, a gentle, quiet life. Didn't you ever want to leave?" And he said, "Not really." And so she says, "Well, like, aren't you curious about the city?" And he says, "No." And she says, "Well, do you ever go down to Edmonton?" And he goes, "Oh, I go down once or twice a year, and I get, you know, some new clothes and a haircut, and, maybe I'll go to a concert or a hockey game." And she goes, "Well, do you ever travel with anyone?" And he said, "No, I just go by myself." And she says, "So have you always been a loner?" And he goes, "Well, kind of." And so she says, "The thing is—I'm just, I'm sitting here with you, and I realize I've known you my whole life, but I don't really know you." And he says, "Well, I'm hoping that will change tonight."

And so they started to talk, and they started to visit, and they went back through elementary and PWK High School memories and all this other stuff, all the experiences they'd shared. But she got to see it through his eyes. And she learned he'd had a really rough time growing up. He was bullied a lot. He wasn't very athletic. You know, Smith is a hockey town; it's a baseball town. And he'd never really wanted to party. Jimmy was never into smoking, or drinking, or toking, or anything like that. He liked his country music, he told her, like George Jones, and Hank, and, you know, the oldies and the goldies.

And so they had the most beautiful meal, and apparently he insisted they get warm apple pie and ice cream and coffee. And they were just—on this island, together. And she started thinking, *This could be it. This could be the one. And he was here all along. How could I have missed Jimmy?*

So, finally, now, he says, "Well, can I give you a ride in my truck?" And she says, "Sure. Where do you wanna go?" And he goes, "Well, you wanna go for a cruise to the landslide, or you want me to drop you off at home, or you wanna come back to my place?" And she says, "Do you live in the back of the hardware store or behind it?" And he said, "Oh, I live on—I live above the, you know, the, uh, store." And she goes, "You live on top of there?" And he says, "Oh, it's beautiful. I've got a wide-open concept, and I've got a big-screen TV, and I can see the church, and the northern lights, and I can look over and see the banks of the Slave River. I can't see the Sky People from my window, but it's still pretty sweet." And she said, "Are you serious? I had no idea that there was a home above there." And he goes, "Oh, it makes sense. People try and break in all the time now." She says, "I didn't know that." And he says, "Oh, yeah. So any time I hear somebody messing around I go runnin' down there. I got a bullhorn, and I usually scare people away. Most of the town here, they're pretty good, but, you know, every once in a while you get people who are drinking, and they're trying to get into the cash register, and, you know, drugs are really big in our town now." And she said, "Oh, I had no idea. Well, I gotta see your house. I wanna see how you decorate." And he says, "Okay."

So they drive to his house and then they get out and he says, "Well, let me go up and I'll turn on all the lights for you and I'll call you." So she waited at the bottom of the stairs around the back. And she's like, "Son of a gun. Well, now I'll find out. Is he a hoarder? Is he cheap? Is his place stinky?"

Pretty soon he calls down, "Okay, come up!" And so she goes up, and he'd lit candles all the way up the stairs. I guess he'd already had them prepared, and he lit them with one of those little barbecue lighters. And there were hundreds of Christmas lights set up in his place too. She said it was a lovely home. And it was wide open, like, you could see the futon, you could see his kitchen. It was all clean, and I guess he had pictures of our leaders, you know, taken through the years, that he'd had framed. It turned out he really loved our little town. He was like a little quiet historian. And she said you could hear the rapids really well from there.

And so she says to him, "I love your place. I'm just so pleasantly surprised," and he says, "Well, do you wanna have more coffee, or do you wanna have, like, some water? I don't really drink juice or anything." And she says, "Well, maybe just a glass of water." And he says, "Why don't you go have a shower?"

Well, she was shocked. And she says, "Have a shower?" And he goes, "Yeah, why don't you go have a shower?" And she says, "Well, why don't *you* go have a shower, Jimmy?" And he goes, "Oh, I already had a shower, right before our feast."

I guess she thought for a minute. Then she says, "Okay, so you realize that if I have a shower in your bathroom, we're not goin' back from that?" And he goes, "That's what I'm counting on."

Then he says, "I love my women all showered up and fresh." She says, "*My women*, no less! How many women have you had?" And he says, "Oh, not too many, but I know what I like, and I like you."

She thought about this, she told me. It was a long time since she'd been with anyone, and every day could be our last with what's happening now in the world.

"Okay," she says finally. "I'm gonna go have a shower, and when I come out, I'm gonna be wearing a towel. And what are you gonna be wearing?" And he says, "You'll find out" and he winked, no less!

So she goes and has a shower, and she's like, "I can't believe that I'm having a shower on top of the hardware store in Fort Smith. I'm about to come out, and we're gonna see what's gonna happen." And then she thought, *Wait a minute! What if Jimmy's a pervert and he's got cameras all set up?* And she thought, *Ah, forget it. Who cares, right? There's aliens in the frickin' sky, so who cares if there's a recording of me towelling off?* So she has a shower, and she gets all gussied up in a towel, and she comes around the corner and he was naked on the bed.

So here's what happened next: they didn't actually go to second or third base. That's what she told us, anyways. They kissed; they held each other; they spooned. She called us early the next morning to prove she had woken up in her own bed, and she said to us, "I need your advice." We put her on speakerphone: "Oh my God, what?" And she said, "Jimmy's different." All us aunties looked at each other with bug eyes, and our perms from '82 almost popped back. "What do you mean? Was he rough? Was he mean to you?"

And she said, "No, not at all."

So we said, "Well, what? Tell us. Like, should we call the cops? Do you want us to get Flinch to go over there and beat him up?"

And she said, "No, he's—he's *beautiful*."

And we said, "Well, like, what do you mean?" We're trappers' daughters, so we're curious about everything, hey?

And so she said, "There are no words for what he is, but he's so beautiful."

And one of my sisters said, "Oh, sweetie. Is he really big? You know what, honey? I had one of those once, and you just, you just breathe. You just pick a point on the wall and you just focus and you just *breathe*. You just...

you just breathe and it's like reverse Lamaze, and you just gotta breathe and push through it. Your body will accommodate."

"Gross, Aunty!" my niece said. "I'm gonna hang up now, because this is not what I was going for."

Giggles, nose snorts and squeals lit up our phone lines as we started texting each other, going, "Stagaatz!", "Mah!" and "Holee!" But the official Aunty message was the same: "Okay, call us back tomorrow when you've had a good sleep," we said.

So she called her best friend, Roberta, I guess. And she said to her, "I need your advice. I really need your help." And Roberta says, "What happened? What what what?" And she says, "Jimmy is ... he's really different. I've never been in this situation before." And Roberta says, "Oh my god. Jimmy's hung like a horse? Because if he is, he doesn't need a little thing like you. He needs a woman like me, okay? I have birthed *twins*, okay? I can take care of that man. If you're telling me what I think you're telling me—not that it's everything, but it doesn't hurt. Well, sometimes it kinda hurts ... but the key here—"

So, Shandra's kept it a secret since then. She's never told us exactly why Jimmy is so beautiful. But in my mind he's what the Crees say: Aayahkwew, neither man or woman but both. One time I had a dream of them lying together in bed. They were holding each other. In my dream he said the most interesting thing to her. "Do you ever have guests stay at your house?" he said. And she said, "Oh, yeah, all the time. I got cousins, and, you know, my relations. They pass through all the time." And he said,

"Do you always wash the bedding right away?" And she said, "You mean the laundry?" And he went, "Yeah. Do you ever leave it for a couple days?" And she said, "No, I do it as soon as they're gone. In fact, most of our guests are trained. They'll bring their wet towels and their bedding to the laundry room and throw it in the wash."

And then he said to her, "Next time you have someone stay at your house, don't do the bedding." And she said, "Why?" He said, "My grandfather was a shaman. And when you went to see him, if you were fighting cancer, or a broken heart, or leukemia, or TB, he would ask you for your favourite piece of clothing. For men it would be a cap, gauntlets, maybe a shirt. For women it might be a scarf, a shirt, a sweater, a jacket that they'd had for years. He would put that piece of clothing in his pillowcase. They said he could see your life: he could dream your life. He would tell you the next day who or what was making you sick or how you were keeping yourself sick.

And then he said to her, "I did leave Fort Smith once for a summer. I helped out my aunty and uncle in High Level, and they had a little motel. I had the run of the place. New guests wouldn't arrive in until late, and I would always nap in the beds that the previous people had slept in. I would always see their lives." He said to her, "Try it some-time. Wait 'til you see what kind of dreams you can have. People leave their dreams behind."

I had that dream myself after she told me how beautiful Jimmy is, and I think that he is a shaman. I think he's a modern-day shaman living in Fort Smith.

Even though they're not an official couple, my niece

says she'll never be with anyone else. But she's fighting marriage, and she's fighting having children for now, because I think she's trying to decide if she's willing to live with a shaman and someone who's both. What does that mean in our communities right now? It's easy to be persecuted if you're two-spirited, or gay, or transgender, or both, or perhaps something we've never heard of before or a being we've forgotten, even under these new skies.

So that's the story that's on my mind these days, about what kind of love they have. And I want laughter for them. I want children for them, if that's what they want. I want to see them standing together, with me and my sisters, on December 17 at JBT Elementary, rooting for their kids and crying at the same time right along with the rest of us, and with the Star People above helping us all.

Mahsi cho.

Super Indians

Chief Danny has outlasted my dad and popes, prime ministers, premiers. He is old-school down and dirty. And whenever he's off negotiating land claims for "his" people, he won't let anyone go with him. He says it's to save "the beneficiaries" money by travelling alone, but there are rumours he has womens in Ottawa. He's been fighting for land claims twenty-two years now, all by himself. And any time the Feds get close to signing, he backs away and he says, "No! This counterfeit white-man paper is an infringement on our treaty rights. That's it—I can't betray my people!" And then the Band's gotta start all over.

We have an Elder who sits in the Band office: Percy. He comes first thing in the morning for the free coffee, and he carries a list of promises that Chief Danny's made over the years. He'll ask, "Where's the Youth Centre our so-called Chief promised? Where's the Old Folks' Home? Where's the jobs?" One time he yelled, "Chief Danny is a negotiator, all right. He's very good at what he does. When you settle your land claims, you negotiate yourself out of a job. He doesn't want that. He likes the cushy life. He likes hopping on a plane every Tuesday to Ottawa, I guess."

Chief Danny always comes in the office from the back, and he leaves from the back too. The receptionist, Clora, has codes for him. I can see her texting whenever Chief Danny pulls up in his truck. If Percy's there, Chief Danny takes off.

And when I think about it, it seems the Band is always in court. I wonder where we get all this money for court fees and lawyers. I've seen the stack of bills. They never stop. And now Chief Danny wants a hydroelectric dam on the Slave River.

Everyone's like, "No! We've got pelicans! We've got sandhill cranes. We've got whooping cranes and arctic lamprey. It's such a fragile ecosystem. We don't need a dam."

But Chief Danny comes from a huge family. Whenever other people or the press raise a stink about his plans, all he has to do is pick up the phone and eighty of his cousins show up, which means he always wins everything. It's cheap. So he's revered by some, hated by others, but bottom line he's like a bulldog wolverine: he's just frickin' fearless. Keep in mind that his self-appointed portfolio is Culture and Lands Protection and Environment. He's the one who decides who "the beneficiaries" are, and if you're against him, you're out.

When you go back through the Band archives, it seems like Chief Danny's always been there, wearing his little moosehide vest and his little black jeans and his little white socks and black running shoes. That's what they call an Indian tuxedo. And—*Wah!*—he has this little knife attached to his belt like he's going to go check his nets sometime soon.

When he travels to these meetings in Ottawa, he goes the extra Native mile with a black leather jacket, moccasin rubbers covering up his moggies that he got in Arizona 'cause they're certainly not our style, a little white shirt that's been washed a hundred times, probably from West Edmonton Mall, and a gorgeous turquoise watch. He's got a mullet, right? Holy, his hair and sideburns practically whistle when they catch the wind while he struts. And he has a truck: a super-modified something that's just loud. He cruises around with his double mufflers, and he blasts the powwow music, boy. He has two coyote tails that trail off the antennae and—get this—BAD TO THE BONE stencilled on one side of his truck and HOOCHIE COOCHIE MAN on the other.

We're all like "Take it frickin' easy!" every time he passes by.

I think you know him or someone like him: traditional but cagey?

Me? I'm Dene Cho: a Tłı̨chǫ daydreamer. I was born here. My late dad was the town mayor and now my mom is. What I love most about Fort Simmer is we're small enough that anyone can make a difference. I really feel that now. I had a rough patch last year. I did not know what to do with my life as everyone else took off for college or university, work, jobs, sweethearts. Sometimes I'd wake up and pray for the day to fast-forward so I could go back to sleep. It was my mom who got me a summer job at the Band office scanning five thousand photos from the Roman Catholic Diocese, who finally mailed them to us from Yellowknife. I'm digitizing them and entering the info that's handwritten on the back. It's incredible. I can see the pride in the families back then. I can feel the dignity and strength and happiness in the portraits of our ancestors. I can see proof of how we used to help one another, though I sure don't see that anymore. People used to farm here; all the portraits show families together out on the land. Everyone had dogs. Everyone looked so strong.

So I'm organizing the archives and the Band library and uploading scanned images on Facebook and our town website. Each upload gets me two hundred likes in the first hour and at least sixty-three shares every day. There are pictures of baptisms, marriages, visits from prime ministers and the Pope. I also help move the tables the Band office rents out for dances and meetings. That wasn't in my job description, but it gets me outside and I get to use the Band truck. It's the little things that are huge for me.

I'm sure it's raised some eyebrows: the mayor's son working here as a Tłı̨chǫ when the Chief and the membership are Bush Cree. But the truth is you can make more money fighting fires or picking morels, so that's what most of the membership does. Smart. I have my own reasons for being here: with access to the archives and computers, I can print up my favourite artwork on the printers we use for maps and signs: like Steven Paul Judd, who does the Hulk with braids, or Ryan Singer's Diné *Star Wars* series. I've printed them up huge for my office. I'm also trying to find more pictures of my dad from when he was mayor here in the eighties. So far, I've found two. People say I walk and stand just like him. Well ...

I just can't help but think that this Band could be doing better. They've got departments for Community Programs, Community Services and Corporate Services. Each of these is run by people who Facebook and plan their next vacation all day long. There's never money for a language retreat or cultural immersion camps, but there's always money for conferences in Hawaii or staff retreats in Vegas, or hand-games tournaments. It's a Band-Aids and Bingos approach to what I worry is for a language and way of life that is slowly dying.

Because Chief Danny is always gone, he sometimes forgets that he's organized these big things, right, and that we have to actually see them through. Like Idle No More. On the day of it, he's like "'Kay! We're blockin' off downtown," and all the other Indians in town were mad, like, "Okay, I need to get my kids from daycare. I'm going through your barricade." Other Natives were like, "Ummm, I gotta check the mail. I'm going to check my mail. I'd like to see you try and stop me from checking the mail." Others were, "Yeah, I gotta get my Nevadas from the Quick Stop," "I gotta get my pop and chips," "I gotta get my diabetes," "I gotta check out the government workers 'cause two of them are recently divorced," "I gotta ..." Chief Danny got mad, and he said, "No! We gotta keep the circle strong!" But, like, there's some pretty tough Indians in our town going, "I'm getting my kid. You coulda done the barricade somewhere else. There's only one four-way in our community and you blocked it?"

"Yeah. We blocked it," Chief Danny said. "And we are blocking it *for you.*"

"Whatever," Iron Steve said. "I'm going through—now." He did, and then everyone drove through honking and, yeah, so that didn't really work out. And there I was standing with a few of Chief Danny's staff with signs that said IDLE NO MORE; WATER IS LIFE; and TAKE MY RIGHTS AND GET A BANNOCK SLAP! I was thinking the whole time: *This is so dumb. It's the cheapest anything. This whole town is lame.*

"Fuck sakes anyways," Chief Danny said. "We are a colonized people. Everyone, back to work!"

Anyway, the story I want to gift you is what happened a couple days ago in our community. See, Chief Danny's had it up to here with the RCMP and the town's volunteer firefighters. I don't know why exactly, but something happened with zoning and his log house, apparently. Chief Danny has a property so huge that his house looks like a fortified log castle. They say you can see it from the plane as you approach the airport. He keeps buying more land too. Supposedly, he has motion-sensing lights and a gate all around his property. He has solar panels on the roof and a water fountain and even a garage filled with pinball machines from the old Ray's Arcade that were repaired on the Band's dime but suddenly disappeared when Ray's went under (a.k.a. was raided for drugs). Our old youth worker is now the prime drug dealer in town, and that's just sad. Whatever.

"The Chief's too good to live in town, I guess." I heard someone say that once. Maybe it was me. Who knows?

This town loves to Hawaiian Hotbox. In case you don't know what that is, it's when you're too poor to go to Hawaii, so you sit in the bathroom with your buds and crank the shower and turn it all the way on hot but don't turn on the fan so the room gets hotter and the humidity index rises and you sit there and pass doobies around and laugh and sweat and your hair gets matted and you can smell the toothpaste and shampoo and it's actually quite nice. Yeah, they say the truth always comes out in the bush or when you're in Rehab or when you Hawaiian Hotbox with your cousins.

So, at this recent meeting with the RCMP and the Volunteer Fire Department—and shall I mention this was a meeting where we were supposed to honour them—Chief Danny said, "Okay, on Canada Day, what we're gonna do is we're gonna have a big tug-o'-war. Okay? And what we're gonna do is we're gonna have the Band Council, all twenty-six of us, we're gonna down your little moonyow RCMP and your little moonyow volunteer firefighters, okay? We're gonna show you that this is Treaty 8 Territory—unceded and unsurrendered, okay? Signed in 1899—okay? Sovereignty, Cousins! We're gonna fly you moonyows back to England for free—you hear me? And halfway there, you're gonna be flying through the air into that big mud pit and you will realize just exactly who the boss is around here. Okay!"

Did I mention that he likes to talk like *Scarface* when he gets going? What. Ever!

We, the employees of the Fort Simmer Band office, side-eyed each other. We telepathically texted each other,

"Holee. No backing down now, hey! What can we do?"

And the Chief kept going: "We're gonna get one of my favourite beneficiaries, Sheri Blaze, out with the firehose to spray down the track. There's gonna be gravel and clay and mud in that pit, probably a couple stolen bikes down there, and you guys are going in, okay?" He flipped a table—WWF style—before storming out. He got in his truck, peeled out of the driveway and sped out of town with those two tails flying in the wind along with his mullet, just Tribe Called Red'ing it all the way to his home to go steal my high score in Galaga, I guess. Lame.

I was like, "So much for reconciliation."

The RCMP looked at the volunteer firefighters, who looked back, and they all started clapping their hands and smiling. "This is going to be so awesome. It is on!"

I saw them trying not to laugh at the Chief directly, but the challenge was out there, and I was embarrassed that people who risked their lives for us had been insulted by Chief Danny. From then on, people got fired up. The wives and husbands and kids of every Mountie and volunteer firefighter were like, "You show them. You show them who they're dealing with."

It was personal. For everyone. Suddenly this became our everything. I got scared. I even did a couple push-ups at home for conditioning, but they hurt so I stopped.

Musta been a Tuesday when Chief Danny took off again to Ottawa to do his thing: negotiate, drink, play pool, negotiate, right? Always in meetings at The Keg, I guess, with a T-bone steak, garlic mash and all the fixin's. *What the fuck ever.*

Yeah right, I thought. Chief, you're busy watching all three *X-Men* movies on Air Canada all the way to Ottawa for the second time this month. He's off and we're organizing this huge tug-of-war. Or I am. Everyone in the Band office except me is still booking their next vacation to Cabo and creeping everyone in town on Facebook.

The Chief arrives back right on Canada Day. He comes in to work and he's like, "Hey, what's this? You a Super Indian, or what?" he says, looking at my office walls. I had printed and hung a pile of new *Star Wars* artwork while he was away: Ryan Singer, Kelly Kerrigan, Andy Everson, Steven Paul Judd.

"Hi," I say. "Welcome back."

I can tell what he's thinking: *You're Tłı̨chǫ. Your mom's the mayor. Your dad was the mayor. Why do you work here? Who's paying you? What are you worth to me?*

"Nobody else at work?" he asked. "What's this—cat's away, mice are gonna play? Where is everybody? There's only two holidays here: baby Jesus' birthday and Aboriginal Day, June 21st. As far as I know, it's only Moonyow Day today, okay?"

I waited, because I could see how this whole thing was gonna go.

He ignored me as he sent out a volley of messages on his two cellphones. I'm going to say that again—he has two cellphones: a new iPhone and a new BlackBerry, both on his belt, right next to his Big Chief Snuffleupagus knife that he uses to slice eight balls of hash for the one-man dance party at his mansion in the bush, I guess.

I said, "Sir, remember that big tug-o'-war you announced for the town?"

And he goes, "What? Yes. Yeah. I remember that."

I said, "Well, it's right now. The whole town's waiting for you."

He clapped his hands. "It's now? Right on. Let's go right damn now. Okay!"

"Yes, sir!"

So we hop in his truck and we go racin' down to the track. Those little coyote tails on his antennae are flopping all the way down there. I notice a big braid of sweetgrass on his dashboard and, boy, it smells nice. I guess every time the sun hits his cab, the fragrance of the land comes rushing in. I can hear the cellphones clipped to his belt rubbing away at his plush seats. When we get out of his truck, everyone's there, right? Everyone's just gettin' ready. They're like, "All right. Here we go. Here we go!"

So, Fort Simmer's population is 2,500, give or take. We're officially five languages. There's Chipewyan, Cree, Tłı̨chǫ, French and English. A beautiful town—a fierce town when it comes to politics, history, pride, love, exes, peace bonds, child support payments, hand games, Nevadas, bingo and hockey, right? The Chief goes racing right up to the front of the tug-of-war line, pushing everyone out of the way. And then—no lie!—he wraps the rope around his body three times.

But what he didn't know was this: two days earlier we'd had a five-hour office party (a.k.a. coffee break). Everyone who was currently standing behind Chief Danny on the tug-of-war line had called for a mutiny of sorts. The

Council members had realized they were doomed. "Man, there's no way we're gonna win against the RCMP and the volunteer fire department. Those guys *live* at the gym. Those guys are on protein shakes and energy bars, and the women are toughest of all, ne'rmind."

Our group looked like little candy apples. How can we all be skinny and fat at the same time? We couldn't possibly win, so the deal was supposed to be that I would stay at the Band office on Canada Day to wait for our fearless leader. I would tell him we had a plan to propose. "How 'bout when they go 'One, two, three,' we all let go? And when the RCMP and the firefighters fall back we can have a good laugh and we'll buy 'em a coffee, and everything will be good, right?"

That was supposed to be the deal. But no one was counting on me, the daydreamer, a.k.a. Super Indian, to decide *not* to tell our Chief about this trick, which had been decided in solidarity just to have a good laugh. And here's why I didn't. Chief Danny is one big stinky loser face. He's always been here, and nothing ever changes. He's made his fortune off of us and our future. Our town looks like a war zone. The Youth Centre is closed all the time; there's no café. The Sportsplex kind of imploded and now the building is condemned. And what do we do? We sit around waiting for something to happen. You know, when I was little, everyone had bush radios on top of their fridges so we could listen to what was happening on the land and hear who needed help or where so-and-so had seen a moose. Now it's police scanners. We're more interested now in who's beating up who, and

I am just so sad when I see the smiles of our ancestors in those photos. I wonder what they would think of us Town Indians living our lives as half of who we could be. Maybe even a quarter. Why the eff am I more excited about looking at pictures of the past rather than looking ahead with hope? These were the ingredients that spurred me in my decision to stage a little mutiny of my own, I guess you could say.

So, as we all lined up for the tug-of-war, Pauline, our secretary, asks me, "Did you tell Danny that we're all gonna drop the rope?"

And I'm like, "Yup. On our way here."

And Dave, our councillor, says, "I dunno, guys. He's wrapped himself up pretty tight in that rope."

I bite my tongue and look down, because this is going to be spectacular.

"Any speeches today, Chief?" the Sergeant asks. Nobody bothers learning their names anymore because RCMP rotate outta here faster than Lady Gaga does a costume change in one of her concerts on YouTube.

"Take our rights," the Chief says, "you're gonna get a flurry of lefts. Let's go!"

We walleye each other and pretend to tighten our grip, but deep down inside we're all like, "Here we go." I'm saying that internally too, but I'm also going, *"Oh my Geaaaaaaaaaaaaaaaawwwd!"*

So, the whole town's there, and they go, "One! Two! Three!" The RCMP and the volunteer firefighters pulled just hard, boy, and we who work at the Fort Simmer Band Council office just let go and Chief frickin' Danny just frickin' flew, boy. It was documented by a hundred cellphones and later posted online in slow motion. Okay: Chief Danny didn't just fly—he uncoiled and spun three complete times in the air as he soared. He flew so fast his little sneakers were still stuck in the mud, and his little white socks. You could see his little white socks as he flew, and his mullet just fanned right out, hey? And what was sad was his little white socks didn't even match.

Yup, about halfway in the air, we saw his eyes bug out and his mouth open before he belly-flopped into the biggest Sarlacc pit of all time. It was mud; it was clay. There *were* a couple stolen bikes in there, and he went *splat*. Also, he had on his leather jacket from The Leather Ranch. He's got his two cellphones, right? His wallet, his glasses. Everything goes into the mud, right? And he's just swimming around, eh? He's just dog-paddling and gulping for air.

And the whole town, they're killing themselves laughing, 'cause they can't believe it, right? Then the publisher for the paper comes up and calls Chief Danny's name, and they hate each other, right? 'Cause the journal's always exposing what the Chief's up to.

And unfortunately—or fortunately, depending on who you talk to—the Chief said the *f*-word just as the picture was taken. You can see him enunciating with his big brown patty-cake face: "Effffffffffffffffuuuuuuu." We all know it's gonna be the cover story, and this little boy comes running up, and goes, "Ha ha ha, Chief Danny! My dad says that you're exactly where you belong. You're just like a pig in—" and the boy said the sh-- word.

And then the Chief yelled something I've thought about every day since. You know what he said? Now, don't forget, this guy is a veteran of the Indian wars, right? What did I say—this Chief survived what? The Pope, prime ministers, premiers? You know what he said to that little boy? He said, "That's no way to talk to your real dad."

At first, everyone thought that was just a bad joke. But then the little boy's mom said, "Danny, *no*!" And that little boy said "Mom—?" and his dad said "Barb—?"

And the woman started to cry.

And Chief Danny crawled out of the mud, grabbed what he could, got into his truck in his little muddy socks, and he drove off. Those little coyote tails just bobbed away in the wind.

And I stood there thinking, *What a thing to do to a little boy: "That's no way to talk to your real dad."*

That poor kid. That poor husband. That poor wife. You know, our Elders say, "There's God's way, there's man's way, there's the Indian way." That's what they say. There's something called Indian court, you know. Brutal, eh? Rugged!

And that was the day I started to plot my revenge. I would spend my life uncolonizing Chief Danny. Seven billion people on this planet and I'd found my reason to live: to take him down and save the North from him and every other loser leader out there. One day I will speak my language. One day I'm gonna raise my family in a good way. I'm going to buy that house Chief Danny's adding onto right now, and I'm gonna reclaim that high score in Galaga that I used to have when I was thirteen.

Chief Danny, your Reign of Cheapness is about to end. My superhero power is now this: I will spend the rest of my life taking you down. I'm going to end you, Hoochie Coochie Man. Here comes the pain from the Tłįchǫ day-dreamer. And, holy shit, this is gonna be fun.

Wheetago War 1:
Lying in Bed Together

Warlike, and just what the doctor ordered. Holy cow. What a night! Valentina!

Valentina...

Valentina!

The way she crouched and sank into me as she squeezed the back of my neck and whispered, "I've got you. I've got you."

Her tattoos. She's marked in ways that aren't ours, I think: her legs, arms, feet and hands. And she's scarred: scorch scars on her hip and bruises all over her. Fresh stitches under her left rib. My God! A warrior! The sweep of her hair over my hands as I held on and the growl of me trying to hold back but losing myself to her every time completely. Holy! The hunger for each other. We became the night.

And who knew suffering could be so glorious? What a goddess. Sweet mercy. I am in awe. I had no idea. I am a brand new man and I am hers now. And on today of all days: my last day as a Handi-Bus driver. I'm free. We could hit the city, get her car fixed, rock out. What can I cook her? Porridge, heavy cream, blueberries. Toast. Jam. Oh, I'm going to spoil her.

Last night I fried up some caribou meat with lots of butter and salt, prepared fresh veggies with tons of butter and a swab of minced garlic. I used my couscous from Kaesers, the garlic blend. As I got all three of my pans and my pot going, I boiled up some mint tea, which I had picked myself at Tsu Lake. Oh, she was hungry.

And now she's back, glowing from the bath.

"Shhhhh," she says. She's dressed. Hair wet. Ready to go. Her clothes, in this light, look different. She's used sinew to mend the tears on her light jacket, and there's a symbol that I see now on her right arm: the skull of a caribou. Did she have that last night? And why does she smell like smoke?

"Shhh?" I say and reach out my hand. "Can I make you coffee?"

She shakes her head. "We have to go."

"Where?" I ask. "The Pelican? I can cook for you—"

"No," she says. "We have to leave."

I frown. "And go where?"

She points to the sky.

I wrinkle my nose. "What?"

"Goddamn you," she says, suddenly serious. "Why didn't you listen to me?"

"Listen?" I asked. "I did everything you wanted me to last night."

"No," she says. She hands me the plastic container for

42

my prescription pills. "What are these?"

My pills. I've had the worst splitting headaches this last year. It feels like a 747 is taking off in my head. I almost go into seizure if I don't get to my pills in time. That container was in my bathroom, tucked behind the mirror. Oh no. Don't tell me she's psycho.

"Those? They're for my migraines."

She shakes her head. "Those aren't migraines. That's us trying to reach you."

"Us?" I say. "Who's 'us'?"

She points up. "Us."

"Okay," I say and pull the blankets close. I'm still buck. "What are you talking about?"

"Remember what I said last night?" she asks. "Remember I said you were needed?"

At the dance. Roaring Rapids Hall, a.k.a. Moccasin Square Gardens. I nod.

"And remember how I said you called me?"

I don't want to blow this with her, but I still don't know what she's talking about. "Yes."

"The guys who were after you have all agreed to stand down. Because of me. I showed them something."

Seriously, Gunner and his bros aren't going to beat me up anymore? "Okay," I say. "What did you show them?"

She sits on the bed beside me and places my prescription bottle on the nightstand. "Close your eyes and focus."

I do it.

She places her hand on my head, and I see a series of brutal flashes. I hear hissing.

Footage. How? I'm whipped into another time: footage.

Grainy footage. Something huge—not human—walking through smoke. Screaming. Praying. The *pop pop pop* of guns firing. Screaming. To my left, bodies are rolling in an ocean of froth. Children. Adults. Upside down. Parts of them, rolling with the tide. People running. Praying in all languages. Running. The something not human is hit by bullets and falls, kneels, gets back up. Throws its head back and howls. Keeps walking. Three beings follow. One without arms. Another flying low to the earth, human face, spinning its body around on its neck.

Then a scream that hurts my head and breaks the feed, and a cut to a forest. Nothing is moving. Hundreds of things are standing still, arms up towards the sky. Their backs. Skin is hanging off their backs, and one is ramming a tusk through another one's head. They are humming. It's a low roll, and they're swaying together. Some are hissing. Some are yelling, but it's a cry song. I hear Valentina's voice whispering, "Go go go go." She stands gripping a long spear, and then people are moving. They slow to a crouch, watching carefully a field of beings praying under a full moon.

I take a big breath and I'm in my bedroom. "How did you do that? Did you drug me last night?" I look in her hand for a microchip. I look around the room for a tiny projector. How did she do this to me?

"We warned you," Valentina says. "You were supposed to stop the Tar Sands."

"Me?" I say. "How?"

She sighs. "Not just you. Everyone. We sent dreams back, and we know you received them."

I glance at her hands. What is she holding? Nothing. "Those were nightmares. How did you do that?"

She looks at me. "Our daughter taught me."

I get the shivers. "Our daughter?"

"You and I have a girl. They're scared of her."

"Who? How? Prove it," I say. "You can't do this shit to my head and not have me asking questions. Just talk to me."

She studies me, then points to my jeans on the floor. "You don't believe me? Okay, in your left pocket two days ago was a shell casing, right? Our Dream Throwers put it there ten years from now. Your mark in the future will be your right hand bathed in yellow pollen. You will leave yellow swaths on the trees to signal where an area is safe."

"Safe?" I say. Shit! I *had* found a shell casing in my pocket when I was getting dressed the other day. I'm pretending to not be stunned, but I am. Ten years from now? Dream Throwers? I'd found that shell casing and sniffed it and known it had been left for me. "From who?"

"It's what." She shakes her head. "What's coming is already here."

"Wait. You sound like something out of *The Terminator*. Don't lie about anything. Just tell me."

She looks so tired. "You know what I'm talking about."

"I don't," I say. "Start at the beginning and tell me."

"The world's ammunition lasts three days. That's it. We hold them off for three days, and then they rule the Earth."

"Who?" I ask. "Who do we hold off?"

"Body Eaters." She looks right at me. "The Wheetago."

"The Wheetago," I say. "Okay ... when?"

"When is the year the caribou do not come down from the coast?"

I glance around the room. "It's now. This year. They didn't come down. The Elders just met, and they are worried."

She nods twice. "This is the year the Wheetago War begins."

"Wait a minute. Come on."

"Do you know what I saw three days ago?"

"Three days ago in the future?"

It's supposed to be a joke, but she nods. "I saw Hell. There were hundreds of dancers. All Native. Fancy dancers. Shawl dancers. Button blanket dancers."

I swallow hard. "Go on."

"There were fields of bodies around them, and they were dancing. Some had been dancing for days. It was the older women who lasted, because they had discipline. The younger ones were bleeding through their moccasins. The drummers had had their left feet pulled off, so they kept time with their right. They'd had their eyes sucked out. They were singing blind, and some had their tongues missing."

"My God," I say.

She starts to cry. "What's worse is once they can't dance anymore, the Wheetago—and there so many of them ... so many different kinds now. They can't wait to rip people apart in front of their families."

"Wait. But what are they dancing for?"

"The mother. She is a queen. She eats the dancers and

then gives birth to a Wheetago. She vomits them."

I cover my mouth.

"Hell is coming, and you're a part of it. You're a prayer warrior, and you're also my husband."

I swallow dry as my heart blooms. "What?"

"There's a future war, but not in the way you think. Site C Dam, Muskrat Falls, Standing Rock..."

"What? That's happening now."

"It all goes wrong. It's a set-up."

"For what?" I reach for her arm. She pulls away.

"For the Wheetago and their mother."

"What?

"You will name her The Mother of All Tusks," she says. "She will be born because when they expand the Tar Sands, the workers will uncover a Wheetago that will bite one of the women from the local community. It's all destined."

I close my eyes. *Why does this feel real? Why do I already know this?*

My neck starts to burn from hickeys; my back is shredded from Valentina's claws. I shake my head. No headaches. Holy sweet mercy. Usually by now I'd be gripping my head, rocking back and forth, praying to be thrown into a sea of ice to stop the pain.

"What if you're wrong? What if you're, like, in a coma and dreaming this, or I am?" I thought of that Facebook meme: *What if the adventures of Indiana Jones are the dreams of Han Solo while he's locked up in carbonite?*

"Don't believe me?" she says. "What's coming back has been waiting for global warming for all its many lifetimes, under the ice. It is patient. Starving."

"So, the Wheetago have been doing what all these years?"

"Praying. And they're learning our dances now. They're learning our songs. I have a feeling they want to teach all of this to their children."

I feel the thrush of cold terror blow through me. What do I really know about her? There are rumours that Valentina is a deity, that she is a being of forever, that she'd also come back to witness the signing of the treaties. When was that … 1899 for Treaty 8 in Fitz, 1921 for Treaty 11? She had downed Gunner and his buddies last night to save me from a snapped spine. Last night in the dark we made ferocious love. Holy moley. But is she sane?

"Valentina," I say. "You can't just drop this on someone. I need more proof."

"Okay," she says. "Tell me the story your grandfather told you. The one you never wanted to believe."

I sit up straight. "My grandpa?"

"Tell me," she says, "about what Pierre saw in Fort Fitzgerald when he was a boy."

I remember slowly. "My ehtsèe," I start, "wanted to work with the men in Fort Fitzgerald when he was young. He wanted to help unload the barges. He lied about his age. 'Holy man,' he said, 'they worked you hard, but they fed you good.'"

"This was when?"

"The thirties, I think."

She glances out the window before looking back at me. "Go on. Hurry."

I concentrate. The terror of Grandpa's story starts trickling back.

"As he was walking with the men to receive their work orders, he saw someone chained on a hill. I have seen this hill. It's low and solid. I will never walk on it. This person was chained and staked to the hill face down. An old woman was guarding the person with a piece of long willow. Thick. Like a staff. As they got closer, my grandpa heard people saying, 'Don't look at it.'

"Of course, as he got closer, he snuck a peek.

"The person was shivering, shaking, trembling. He or she had rubbed their own feces into their hair. They'd eaten off their own lips, their own fingers and one whole side of their face. This person looked up at my grandpa and their eyes met. He froze. The being raised its arms off the ground and, as that happened, my grandfather felt the strength leave his body. He collapsed.

"The old woman started whipping the Wheetago and yelled in Cree, 'Let him go!' The unholy beast did. It took my grandfather a full day to feel like himself again. He was so weak after."

Valentina nods. "That was only a glimpse into their power. They can stop shells from firing. As your grandfather saw, they eat their own lips, and most of their fingers. They're always suffering. The more they eat the hungrier they become; the more they drink, the thirstier.

"But in the future—our future—they start to decorate themselves for something. They have Oracles that use animal spit and medicine to kill from a distance. Some have sewn or pushed sticks and antlers into their bodies.

They use ptarmigan bones and suet to tattoo each other. These Wheetago are older than Christ, and they have been counting on our greed as humans to warm the Earth so they can return. That thing on the hill, it was a scout."

"Fuck," I say.

"In the future, we just saw them, you and me and our girl, humming. So many of them, looking at the moon, shivering like bats. Their corridors are growing."

"Corridors?"

"Their range is expanding globally at 144 miles a day."

"Stop," I say. My jaw hurts. I've been grinding my teeth as I listen and dig into her truth. "Okay. Okay. If I believe you, what am I in the future?"

"Besides being my husband?" She runs her hand up my arm. "Because of us, I give birth to one of the greatest Wheetago hunters of all time: our girl." She levels her eyes in the direction of somewhere I don't know. "Now it's time for us to leave this place and begin to train."

"If this is really true," I say, "I need you to do that thing again. No tricks. Bring me your worst memory from the future."

She holds out her hands to me to show me she's holding nothing.

"I'm not sorry you will see this," she says as she places her palms against my ears. I hear a roaring, and I see people picking blackberries along burning hills. Some seem to be walking back to their camp. As I zoom in closer, I see women and men dragging themselves along, carrying buckets. Ahead of them people are kneeling and rolling berries with their fingers to create jam. The people dig into open skulls that are tied to trees, mixing the brains with the berries. These people have no hair, no feet, yet they're still alive. Screaming, drooling, twisting. There are seven creatures on a hill watching them, like priests. Flame flickers above each of their heads. The priests are decorated for war: huge antlers rise from their skulls and throats. At the top of the hill stands a bull Wheetago. It is hunched, huge, trembling in its ferocity. It has the mouth of a hammerhead shark with a thigh bone rammed through its cheeks. The hill it stands on is made of human and animal bodies torn in half and drained.

The Wheetago sniffs to read the wind. *A Patroller.* I somehow know this. The guard hairs around its neck are like those of a big cat. Behind it are more hills made of bodies with more bull Wheetago perched on top like pawns. Shovel Heads, we call them. Patrolling. Guarding. You can hear their bellies boiling if you get close enough to them. Behind them, on the biggest hill of all, I see the Queen. She is a human giant, giving birth to more Wheetago through her mouth, just like Valentina described. Hundreds of other Wheetago approach, holding human heads like chalices served up as offerings, full of brains mixed with blackberries. The Queen licks blood from her mouth and drinks from one skull. Then another. Then another. She looks in my direction. Her eyes say it all: she hates the world and she hates us. She bares her teeth and makes a grabbing motion towards me. She wants her children to kill and eat the world. She holds up a skull. It's upside down. It has the face of Valentina, eyes open.

Mouth torn apart. An ear hanging from a braid. Beside her two Hair Eaters have a girl. The most beautiful little girl I've ever seen. She's like a little Valentina. Golden. One Hair Eater steps on the girl's arms as another rips her legs apart, and I realize this is our girl. "*No!*" I scream. The Mother of All Tusks throws her head back and howls.

The seven priests raise their hands to the sky.

The bulls rake their heads back and forth. As they join this howl, the earth around them moves. The hills of skulls sway.

And I see a flash.

I come back. Ears ringing.

I'm freezing, cold, terrified.

Oh my God. It is the end of the world, and we have caused this by doing nothing.

"See?" Valentina says.

"Was that our daughter?"

She leans down and kisses me. "We have to go."

"Wait," I say. "That was you? You and I ..."

"We have a few years," she says and smiles. Then she's crying. "You can save her. Four Blankets Woman says you can save her, but you have to come now."

"What about you?" I ask.

She looks at me and wipes her eyes. "Don't worry about me. I have another way."

My heart is pounding, and I need water. I try to think. "What is our daughter's name?"

"Ehdze," she says.

"For the moon," I say.

"For moonlight."

"Whoah," I say. I get the tingles. That was always my favourite word in Tłįchǫ.

"Hurry," she says. "Everything starts now. Take my hand and we'll leave. But you can never come back, because there'll be nothing you want to come back to."

I look around. This house. My life. The world I know or knew. I take her hand just to see what will happen. Valentina. The woman who's in all of the photographs of the treaty signings, if you look close enough. Ageless and war-torn.

"Ehdze," I say and get the tingles again. *Moonlight.* I'm going to save our daughter. We're going to change this.

I take my wife's hand.

She squeezes

We vanish

and are reborn into the Full Fleshing: the Return of the Wheetago.

Wheetago War II:
Summoners

You know what happened at Bear House. Three weeks ago…

For the record, I cannot hear much of what you're saying. I've lost most of my hearing in both ears, so I'm just going to start.

No, Sir. I cannot answer that. That is our Clan Business, and you know better. You released the names of those who passed before you should have. There's a fourth sister, and this is how she finds out? After Kateri's through with me, she'll come looking for you. I promise. We have protocol for a reason, and you blew it. Can I start?

I think we all agree that what happened to us out at The Halfway led to the taking of Outpost 5.

For those of you who don't know, we took a bush school on a field trip outside of Outpost 5, at what we call The Halfway. The children could choose either to get porcupine quills with Teacher Norma or to set snares for rabbits and grouse with Yellow Hand, Norma's husband, at

The Gate. The children we were charged with were the group who chose Norma: her daughter, Sarah, and seven other smaller kids. Each was marked in the way of the walrus or the caribou—this signifies if they are guardians of the land or the sea. Each child and teacher wore Silencers around their chests along with life jackets that were brightly lit in case there needed to be a quick evacuation or body Recon.

I remember Norma. Her fierce eyes. How she sang. No song or prayer will ever be whole now without her. I mean that.

"Okay, everyone. Gather round," she said. "Today we're going to learn how to harvest porcupine quills."

I remember Sarah asking, "Mom, is this the trail where the Na acho used to pass?"

Norma nodded. "Yes, my girl. A long time ago, Na acho, the giant ones, used to pass here. See that mountain? Look along the sides. That was all scraped smooth by giant beavers as they made their way south for war."

The kids and us, the guards who were supposed to be protecting them all, looked up in astonishment. You could see the huge scrape on the face of the rock. The Na acho were the ancient ones, the giants that used to roam the Earth: giant beavers, giant eagles. Christ, we could sure use them now.

"Will they ever return?" a girl asked.

"Of course they will," young Sarah said. "With great evil spilling into the world, we have to have faith."

The group quieted at this. We were amazed someone so young could be so wise. Sarah had been spending time with Old Man, the Chanter. I wondered if these were her words or his.

"Dove told us they heard mermaids singing under the ice here last spring," one of the shyer boys said. Amos was his name.

A child named Stephen added: "My mom says Dove is both a girl and a boy."

Who is Dove? Dove's our Shifter. Our Moon Watcher. Yes, Dove is a Shifter. I'll tell you what: after you hear what happened, you won't be rolling your eyes when I mention that name. Can I continue?

So Norma held her hands out. "Okay now. Let's focus on the lesson of today," she said.

She motioned for us to approach the body of a dead porcupine as she pulled on thick gloves. "Here we are. I saw this little one yesterday when we were picking berries. We'll drop tobacco in honour of this little life's passing."

As I scanned the horizon and trees, doing my job, I could smell the fresh smoky tobacco they passed around. The students knew not to distract us. There were four other guards, Kateri's three sisters and a distant man—Stanley, they called him—who could fell a Wheetago from a mile away. Stanley was an ace at using his .30-30 to take out the eyes of a Shovel Head. I saw that myself at least five times.

What happens when a Shovel Head is blinded? The others eat 'im. It's pretty to see Hair Eaters turn on each other like that.

So the teachers and students dropped tobacco and offered it to the earth and to our Mother.

"Today," Norma said, "we give thanks for all we have. My husband's birthday is soon approaching, and I want to make him new moccasins. Our camp is low on beads, but you can use porcupine quills to decorate just about anything if you know what to do. Lucky for all of us, Aunty knows what to do."

The kids beamed. I could feel it. No matter what happened after, I can go back to that last exact perfect moment.

Uncle Ned was with us as well. I'm not sure why he was there. Bored, maybe. Maybe he wanted to feel the sun on his face. Maybe he wanted to watch the children learn. We'll never know now, will we?

The guards: each of us was tattooed, pierced and marked with the sign of the caribou. Two of us had dreadlocks and a side shave. One had her hair tied tightly in a bun. Like the others, each of us had a pair of military-grade Silencers. All it takes is for one Wheetago to scream, and it can freeze the lot of you. I've seen that ... or I should say I've seen what a group of humans looks like after. You never forget it. The Wheetago suck the brains of their victims out through their eyes once the victims are frozen. That means you see your murderer coming. You can't do a thing.

We were armed with Decapitators, flares, machetes, handguns, rifles. I'd left my Decapitator at home that day, thinking I had enough with my rifle, side piece and flare gun. Stupid. Stupid. Stupid. *Stupid.*

It was a beautiful day. The leaves were yellow, gold. Frost had been on the grass earlier that morning. No wind. You could hear for miles.

I thought I saw movement out of the corner of my eye. My hunting glasses: if a bird passes, those glasses catch the reflection. When I'm hyper-aware, I move quick. We all turned. Nothing.

Can we come back to this later? Why? 'Cause I have a theory, that's why.

Norma showed Sarah and the other students how to take care in pulling out the porcupine quills with a tool she'd built. They were pliers she'd modified. I took the time to admire the shawls that Norma and her daughter wore. Norma's shawl covered her belly and had a caribou on it. Sarah's had a caribou as well, but it was a young one. Innocent. The women, they had started loomin', and what they were turning out was beautiful. It brought hope, which is a dangerous but welcome thing. We were all feeling human again. Norma was pregnant, eight months. And here she was with her daughter preparing gifts for Yellow Hand's birthday. I thought to make him one of my famous T knives. They're small but lethal.

On this expedition, Sarah was the oldest. I can say I truly knew only three of the smaller ones. The Outpost was growing. We had hope. Strength in numbers. My three little buddies were Tyler the Blond, Alex the Bulldog and Shane the Fearless. Those were my names for them.

I remember laughter. Uncle Ned was smiling at the time. He looked young; his face was clear, radiant. He looked at the twin suns before he met my eyes. I admired his braids, how his wife had wound stained moosehide into them. He always carried his Silencers around his throat. All he'd need to do was duck and they'd be on in a heartbeat. I'd copied him the second I noticed the way he had shaved them down and covered them with moose—

Then Ned winced. I recall watching him. His face twitched. That was when it happened. He winced when he saw how one of the guards—Old Mah—looked at a bird on the ground with its wings fanned out. It was a magpie. Old Mah was still wearing her teddy bear in a baby carrier. She had lost her baby. You know the Wheetago. One of their priests—or Oracles, as you call them—had sewn what was left of her boy into the bark of a tree.

The bird was face down on the earth—alive—with its wings fanned out. *It's eating something,* I thought. I remember that. We looked further. I drew my gun. There were six other birds like that. Face down. Wings out. Raking their beaks into the earth to eat something.

Old Mah asked, "What is it?"

Ned made a joke: "Even the birds are praying now."

One of the birds turned its head to look up at us. A calligraphy of light—pure blue fire—erupted from between its eyes as it rose into the air and spun.

What we had witnessed was over, but something cold flashed through me: *Summoners.*

They were calling something forward.

All seven birds exploded into flight.

Uncle Ned shouted, "We need to leave this place—*now!*"

I looked over at our group: Norma, wearing special gloves, was holding the porcupine. She was pulling a quill out. Sarah was beside her, holding out a bag for her mom.

Then it sprang back to life. The porcupine just came back to life in her hands. It wasn't dead at all. Or maybe it was, and this was a spell. Either way, it was a trap.

Its eyes. They looked like eggs boiled to death.

The porcupine grabbed Norma's ears with its paws and tore her face apart in front of all of us.

I saw the faces around me: pure horror.

The porcupine hissed at us with pure hatred.

I heard a click from Uncle's gun behind me. Then another. And another. Ned pushed me forward and yelled, "Shoot that thing! My gun's jammed!" But I couldn't. Norma's shawl hung open. Her belly. The baby. I couldn't locate the target with all the blood that was flying. I did not want to hit Sarah or that baby inside Norma. *Save the baby*, I kept thinking. *Save Sarah and the baby. I'm sorry, Yellow Hand. It's too late for your wife.*

"Save the children!" someone yelled. "Back to the Outpost!"

"Norma, you fight it," Uncle Ned shouted. "Think of Sarah and your little one on the way. Fight it, so Sarah can run to us. Somebody, shoot that creature!"

The porcupine hissed again. Blood streamed down Norma's arms, her neck. It was a blur of ripping, quills, tearing. Her hair flew. Chunks of it. Norma's spine snapped as she bent backwards. Now we knew the Wheetago spirit had her.

Ned shoved me again. "Shoot it, goddamn you. She's Wheetago now. Kill her and that thing before it gets all of us." His pistol was by his feet. He'd tossed it there after it wouldn't fire. He'd drawn his rifle but it dry-fired, and he tossed that too.

The problem with kids is that, as many drills as we go

through with them, they all run off in different directions. Who can blame them? We were all terrified. I heard the safety going off on my rifle as I aimed to fire.

I heard Sarah yell, "Mom?"

Click—

My rifle jammed.

Click—

I kept pulling the trigger. What should have been two skull shots was nothing instead.

Ned yelled for Sarah to come. She bolted towards him. "Uncle!"

I dropped my rifle and pulled out my pistol. *Click*—

Again. Nothing was working. The other guards were all in shock: none of our guns were firing.

Norma shot back upright but crooked, looking at all of us. The only way I can describe it? It's like it came from behind her. Her face started to boil. She had left, and something else had come back. Something else bore through her. She had turned Wheetago. She advanced towards us, all hunched up, taking a huge breath ...

"Shit!" I yelled. "Silencers! Do not let her scream." I dropped my pistol, ducked into my Silencers and pulled out my flare gun. I decided to aim for her mouth before she could bite us or let out one of their Hell cries.

But then she did the strangest thing. She found the sharpest rock jutting upwards and slammed her face on it over and over, splitting her jaw in half, breaking her teeth into a maw of fangs.

I couldn't risk looking behind me. I used my shoulder to prop my Silencer open. "Who has the children?"

"Got 'em!" one of the sister guards yelled.

"Get them back to the Outpost and send help!"

As I brought my shoulder up, my right Silencer flipped open. I could not get it back down.

Sarah, who had been with Uncle Ned, darted back towards her mother.

I could hear that Ned was frantic. "Sarah, put on your Silencers! Stay away from your mother! She's not herself anymore!"

Norma and the porcupine spotted Sarah at the same time. We had never seen anyone Turn with a baby still inside them. Norma's face was a bleeding skull watching her daughter, and I could tell she was getting ready to bite. The porcupine lunged.

Somebody yelled. A yell of fear. I looked and saw that three of the guards were under attack. What had them had come from above. A rope of guts sprayed out from one of the sisters. Aggie, her name was. That rope was as long as her braids. This Wheetago looked like a new kind: a Reaper, I believe they call it. With the beak.

The porcupine was mid-air when an arrow nailed its head to a tree. The arrow had been fired by Dove, the Shifter, who was by luck returning with two jugs of fresh water just then.

Dove's Silencers were still around Dove's throat. I remember that.

Norma charged towards Dove.

Dove flipped a Decapitator and caught Norma perfectly by the throat. She was immobilized for now, clawing the air. And she could not scream.

The way Dove caught her was amazing.

I pulled my machete out and headed for Norma. This had to be quick.

And that was when we were hit with the grenade.

It tore Ned in half and knocked me out. Dove too.

I must have been out for a good five minutes. When I woke up, I was covered in what was left of Ned. The sisters and Stanley had been pulled in half and eaten. Splitters had gotten to them. If you don't know … it's a horrible thing to witness. They'd been skinned and gutted. Some Wheetago choke on moose fat. We've yet to see if this works on Splitters. Oracles? Yes. We've seen them gag on moose fat and drop. So far, none have resurrected themselves.

The children were gone too. Even Norma's baby. They'd taken the children and the one who was wanting to be born. They were all gone.

Oh. My theory? They say that Earth had seven billion humans before the Wheetago returned, right? I think that was the Wheetago's magic number. Men warmed the world and the Wheetago unthawed themselves from whatever Hell they were in. I think seven billion was the magic number for the amount of meat they'd need to make the world maggoty with them and their kind.

Maybe the Wheetago Turned God too. Who knows?

Sure. Fuck. I could eat a bullet. Millions have. But I think of this as a game now. Something's happening. Something bigger than all of us. Even them. It's an awakening. I think if I make it, I'm gonna witness an answer to all our prayers.

Are four horsemen gonna come racing across the sky?

Are we gonna hear the trumpets over their screams?

Or was the world always theirs? Have we been praying to the wrong God all this time?

As sure as something made all of us, I want to see what's gonna happen next. Because who do they worship? Do you ever think of that? When they're swaying together there under the moon like stalks of wheat, who are they praying to?

Those birds were Summoners. They or an Oracle called a spell on that porcupine to trick us. And the Wheetago can freeze guns. It's happened before, but not in the numbers that happened to us. Their power is growing. They're problem-solving, and now they can sense electricity. If they're using their magic, what do we have? We have Old Man and Iris, his wife. We have Dove. I have to believe that the magic the Wheetago have, that reciprocal magic or medicine, I have to believe that some of it's coming our way. Because otherwise, how do you explain what the Old Man and Iris can do? You can't. And we have Dove. I am here to nominate Dove for the Mark of the Butterfly. You bet your ass I am. Dove goddamned saved me. I pray they wake up soon from that coma. But the Wheetago won't be forgetting Dove.

Why do the Wheetago want our children? It ain't killing. It's something more. Something... for their rituals. We've seen their altars out there on the land. Some of our scouts have seen them smudging with human hair. Are they calling on something through our children? What if there is something bigger coming?

I've only seen a few kinds of them: Hair Eaters, Shark Mouths, Boiled Faces. Yellow Hand saw one that could fly. I have seen Shovel Heads. They're slow, but they ain't stupid, and it takes a lot of stabbing to take one of them down, never mind a herd of them. They eat everything in their path. But an Oracle? One of their wizards? No. We've heard reports of the flames above them when they walk. I saw that fire over the porcupine's head, and the magpie's. I don't know what to think of that.

But what if they want our children ... like ... to make them? We know from reports that their Mother births more Wheetago from her mouth. That's how Wheetago are made. Unless you're bitten. Then it's all over. You're Turned.

But one of them kids: Shane. He was my godson. I have to walk by his grandmother every day now. I would have gladly given my life for his, but when there are no bodies there's no peace.

So where are they? Where are those kids? What if they're raising them as their own?

I sit here before you to say that I will lead any excursion back to the Outpost. You need a scout? I'm your man. We must preserve everything there to maintain what we have left. Because we have to take back our kingdom. But first things first: we have to find our children.

That grenade? It could have been thrown by a human working for the Wheetago. Yes, I've heard of the farms in the South. I can't think of anyone in our camp who would have something like that. And where are my Silencers and the Silencers of Uncle Ned and Dove? Those

Silencers were gone when we woke up. Also, some of our magazines. The Wheetago don't use our weapons. I don't think they know how. But if it was humans helping them...

I recognized Shane's armband on the grass beside me when I woke up. I was there when it was given to him in ceremony, and I carry it with me now. I took it to Old Man. He prayed on it. He said Shane's still alive, and I believe it. I had given Shane a knife just that morning. One I made. I have to believe that boy is alive. I need to believe it. Earth ain't ours anymore. I can feel it every day since the Three Day War. That's all it took: three days to claim a God and a planet?

Maybe we had it coming.

But whatever time I got left on this planet, I'm gonna use it to get those kids back for their families, for our larger family. Count me in.

Mahsi.

The Promise

The wedding was going as planned. The food was great. Most everyone had made it to the hall. A few people got lost but, well, they showed up for the smorg. It hadn't snowed, as we'd worried. It was our night. Finally, husband and wife. Finally!

We were at the head table. Gifts, despite us saying we didn't want any, kept piling up around us. We smiled and shook our heads. After about ten requests, Carly and I kissed and danced. Then we started making our rounds, thanking as many people as possible.

It was when I made it back to the head table first that my buddy Hank came up, shook my hand, leaned in and whispered, "Remember the promise."

He smiled, patted my shoulder and waded his way back to the smorg.

The promise: Lord, I have never forgotten.

I closed my eyes and let this ditty of a doozy roll back into my psyche full throttle.

* * *

It was a Pro-D Day in Fort Smith, 1986. Halley's Comet had returned from her seventy-six-year orbit. Mr. Mister's "Broken Wings" was playing on CBC. I had told Hank that we had the new Intellivision game *B-17 Bomber* at our place, but we didn't. He showed up all ready to rock and spend the day eating hoagies and Fig Newtons (our fave) and drinking Jolt Colas, but it was a trick. I had none of these. What I did have was some work gloves, my dad's coveralls and two pairs of steel-toed boots. "Get to work," I instructed him.

"Where's the new game?" he asked, worried, with frog eyes. "And the grub? This is our day!"

"Don't worry about it," I said. "Soon, Dog Brother. Soon."

He looked at me lopsided. "This better not be a trick."

"Me? Naw," I said. "Let's go."

So we worked. Well, actually, I monitored while Hank worked. I vied for an Academy Award by making a show of how heavy the snow in the driveway was. After shovelling, Hank hauled and poured load after load of wood into our woodbox, so excited about the new Intellivision game.

"Crom, count the dead!" I roared as I pulled out my daddy's jumbo axe and started splitting the monster stumps.

I didn't have the heart to tell him. Wally's Drugs was sold out of *B-17*s, and I had been too lazy the night before to zip to Kelly's to buy the goodies that were supposed to get us through the day.

Man, I worked him. After the woodbox and the shovelling, it was vacuuming, doing dishes, washing walls, scrubbing toilets.

Hank and I were both only children, so we'd adopted each other as brothers. We mostly got along, but every once in a while I pulled the elder card. Today was one of those days. My mom had given me a list of all the chores I had to finish by the time she got home. I'd been on a lazy streak the past month. Maybe I was growing too fast. Maybe I was obsessed with the way the blonde—definitely not Michelle Pfeiffer—shimmied on the screen in *Grease 2*. Who knows?

Either way, once the chores were done, Hank was devastated to learn all of the things I'd promised were pure fibs.

"Fuck sakes," he guppied.

"Sorry," I said and opened my palms. "I don't know what to say."

"Are you serious?" he mewled. "We don't have *B-17 Bomber*?"

I shook my head. "Nope."

"And you don't got hoagies?"

Shook my head again.

"Jolt?"

I shrugged and shot him the best line out of *Fast Times at Ridgemont High*: "Can't give you what I don't have."

I actually saw his eye sockets bulge. "How bone. This is the worst day ever."

I smiled. "It's the best. Look at my house. It's clean and the chores are done."

I got the giggles, and my feet started to sweat. I almost had to bite my palm to stop from braying like a donkey'd hyena.

71

"This fuckin' sucks," Hank said. "I trusted you."

"Dude," I said. "I'm the victim here. How do you think I feel?"

He looked at me. "I'm going home. This coulda been the greatest."

He was reaching for his *Edmonton Journal* sidesack when I looked at the clock. My mom wouldn't be home for another fifteen minutes.

"Okay, okay," I said. "How about we play rock, paper, scissors—best out of three—and, whoever wins gets to do the ultimate WWF move on the other guy and then the loser has to submit and then we flip it, so everyone gets a turn."

He put his bag down. "No illegal moves?"

I shook my head. "No illegal moves. Are you kidding me? They're, like, illegal."

He looked at me. I sensed some good-hearted vengeance in him.

"Let's go."

I got my hand ready for rock, paper, scissors, and we went for it. I won the first time, the second time, the third time. It made no sense. Some things can't be explained.

"Shit!" Hank said and pointed at me. "No illegal moves."

"As if," I shrugged. "She never crossed my mind."

He got into a wrestler's stance. "Okay, what's your move?"

Hank had the gene where he could go Berzerker, so I had to watch it. He'd nailed me a few times in the past, kicked me so hard in the grapes that the good lord above waved his holy hands and played the hokey-pokey below my soles as my body flew yonder.

I shook my hand and pointed. "On your tummy," I said. "Arms out. Pretend you're Jesus."

He got down and did as I instructed. "Frick sakes," he said.

I got the jitters then. This was going to be poly-mygorphix. I could see his big brown toe poking out of his sock. We used to be altar boys together, Hank and me. He was wearing an old belt his dad had given him before walking out on his family. I had a moment of pity, but I knelt down and hiked one of his arms over my leg. This had to happen. I had to secure my day as the victor.

"This isn't the Camel Clutch, is it?" he asked me, lookin' back.

"Naw," I said. "That's illegal. Plus, it's panzy ass."

I hiked his other arm over my leg and tried not to laugh.

"This feels like the Camel Clutch," he said.

"Nope," I said and knelt down. "It's a new move I just invented called—*the Camel Clutch*!!"

Holy fuck, boy! I grabbed his neck and pulled back and his little hands started flapping until they turned purple. He bucked as I rode him into the sunset of my dreams. "Oh yeah!" I did my best Macho Man Randy Savage impression and Hopalong Cassidy'd Hank across the carpet. It was so rad! I was a fuck barnacle. I felt great. This was the best day ever.

Until I felt hot soup running down the back of my hands.

"Oh, shit," I said. "Dude, are you drooling on me?"

I looked, and they were tears. Hank was crying. He couldn't breathe. His Adam's apple was seizing. I dropped him fast.

"Fuck!" I said. "Hank, I am so sorry. So so sorry. Shit, dude!"

Hank took the biggest breath of his life and let out a huge soul cry. He cried and cried and cried as I curled up to him like a ref. Like a paramedic. I had only minutes left before my mom came home.

"Hank, *Hank*. Hank! I am so sorry. Hank. I thought you could breathe."

Hank shook his head and cried. I saw three of his toes poking out even farther. They were all beside themselves purple. The oxygen couldn't reach them. I noticed how weathered and cracked his dad's belt was. Hank wore it every single day, hoping his dad would come back—that fuckin' cock knocker. My brother cried and cried.

I felt horrible. I'd pulled a trigger. Worse, my mom was on her way home soon, and I'd be grounded if she saw what I'd done to Hank. The rule in our house was "No wrestling. None at all." Not to mention illegal moves. Mom knew what was illegal because she had a crush on Ricky Steamboat.

I got an idea.

"Hank!" I yelled. "It's your turn. You can do it to me. Do it. Do the Camel Clutch. Frickin' snap my back, bro."

I'd said it, but I was puzzled. Why would I invite such a thing? Oh, yeah: so I wouldn't get grounded. Plus, I was older and stronger than Hank. I'd just pretend to cry, like I'd done when I was seven and my mom broke a wooden spoon over my ass. She and I both started laughing afterwards.

I went down Jesus Christ style. "Look! Look at me."

Hank wiped his eyes and looked at me.

"Come on. Hurry! Give me the Camel Clutch, fuck dink!"

Hank stood slowly, shakily, like Godzilla reborn. His eyes bugged. I could see the vein under his left eye, and he was still kind of purple. He started to shake. He made fists. It was only the third time I had ever seen him loaded like jack. "You want me to do it to you?" he roared. "You want me to do it to you?" His soul was a froth.

"Fuck, yeah. Let's see what you got, Donkey Balls."

He hated when I called him Donkey Balls. It dated back to a swimming lessons incident before kindergarten. I sealed my eyes shut to concentrate on what needed to happen. I had to make my reaction look Ace!

Hank hopped on. He yanked my arm up. I heard a pop. That was my shoulder.

I opened my eyes.

He yanked my other arm back. *Pop!*

Fuck, that hurt. Was he slapping handcuffs on me or what?

Then he locked the move, grabbed my throat and sat down, and you know what? *There is no resisting the Camel Clutch!*

I saw stars, and the pain was horrific. I could hear the snap, crackle and pop of my spine as gristle and sinew ripped. All that meat turned inside out in a blender of searing agony, with immediate bone chunks turned into blood slush. My back ribs were crunched and mangled. Hank war-ponied me and dry-humped my carcass. Out of the corner of my snake eyes, I watched my hands turn purple. My voice box froze under my tongue. It was an upside-down porno. All I could see was the bottom of his jaw as he yanked up as hard as he could. Then I saw the tunnel of light.

Heaven is real.

I saw pillars of fire and light.

I saw my grandparents.

I saw my cousin who drowned.

I saw thousands of angels in a chorus, shaking their heads and sweeping their wings along pine-needled floors. They were giving me the ultimate northern tell-off: "Fuck, you guys are dumb. It was a Pro-D Day and you two Jabronies wasted it."

Classic RC stuff: nothing but judgment.

* * *

I came to just as my mom was dropping her work bag. She yelled, "Hank Jesse Sparrow, get off of my son! What are you two doing?"

Oh sweet finger of Judas. Hank dropped me. I fell. He collapsed down beside me, and both of us lay there bawling our heads off. I cried out of gratitude. Cried out of relief. I couldn't feel my left leg at first, but then the hottest, lumpiest blood-curdled meat slush start to rush back to all of the destroyed tissue.

"You're grounded!" Mom yelled. "Both of you! You're

not even allowed to look at each other for a month. You know the rule. No wrestling in this house, and was that an illegal move? That totally looked like an illegal move."

My fingers felt cold. Scary cold. Paralyzed cold. Shit! I thought about how I'd smashed Hank's foot through the drywall after we finished watching WWF's *The Main Event* one night. We got so fired up. Well, actually, I had. Now we just lay there and cried and cried and cried.

Mom put on the water for tea and then called Hank's mom and told her to get over here. "Listen to what your son did to my son!" She dragged the land-line phone over to my bawling mouth, and I hollered for extra effect. I was getting rug burn from all the cavorting.

Hank was beside me, and our heads were touching. What would we do for a month without seeing each other? I let out some more sobs just thinking about it. I couldn't talk yet, but I wanted to claw my way towards him and say, "I'm sorry, Dog Brother. I betrayed you!"

Hank's mom showed up and yanked him limping out the door with his jacket hanging off him. He left behind his canvas *Edmonton Journal* sidesack bag, the one his dad had got him from the city, and later that night I went through it. You know I did. He'd bought us a jumbo bag of Cheezies and two cans of root beer and some Pop Rocks, a.k.a. "Molar Exploders." My second fave. There was also some *Star Wars* chewing gum with cards inside. Why the eff would he not have said he'd brought all the num-nums? I swore I wouldn't dive into the stash until we were reunited, but my resolve only lasted a day, and then I went bananas.

Shit, fuck and damn, that was a long month. We didn't even talk at school. We did look at each other, but there was a force field we couldn't penetrate. Hank was still so mad at me. I had a limp. For serious. My back was fucked. I could see that so was his. We were like two old geezers back from the war.

"Hank!" I'd call.

He'd look at me sideways and steer the long way around to his locker.

It was a misery.

Hank and I had bought each other Garfield calendars from the drugstore the Christmas before. I put a tiny X on mine for the day we could finally be buds again. I knew he was doing that too.

So, a month to the day, he called me—or maybe I called him. Only the sands of time know for sure, but contact was made. Sweet Jesus. Contact was made.

We were like two little turtles stranded on separate islands in the Pacific who looked up to see a Twin Otter flashing its brights to say it had spotted us. It was like that only better.

Hank and I arranged to meet at the rusted elephant slide at the JBT playground. Before he got there, I was already sitting with a diamond willow switch. The clouds were pillowy white. Hank made his way through the bush out into the open. During the past month, I had filled his *Edmonton Journal* bag with replacement everythings. The pops were still cold from Liz's.

Hank, despite himself, smiled his father's smile when he saw me. I smiled too. I diverted blood to my upper lip to amplify my admiration for the moment. It was my turn to look froggy.

A truce.

Fuck, did he have a limp. It was pronounced. Mine was bad, but his was so much worse.

I pulled myself up and hobbled over to him. We hugged. "Frickin' Camel Clutch," he said. We snickered like I imagined horses would—we never had any up here, none that I had seen, anyways.

I motioned that we should sit under the slide, like we always did, in the shade and the light of each other. Even in Heaven we'll meet there, I bet.

I gave him back his bag.

"Sweet. You never touched it?"

I swung my head. "Wouldn't've dreamt of it."

He looked at me when he felt how cold the cans were.

I shrugged.

He popped one and handed it to me.

I waited for him to open his, and then we chugged. We'd eat the Cheezies later, after the *Star Wars* cards were opened. He could have my gum.

"Long month," I said.

He glanced at me and smiled. "Yeah."

We were like convicts just released, already scheming.

"My grades picked up," I offered.

"Mine too."

I leaned sideways into him. "Sorry for everything."

He shook his head and tried to sound like his old man had. "Don't mean nothin'."

"It's fuck all when you think about it," I said.

"You know," he began, but stopped so we could listen to a grasshopper. A sweet hot summer wind enveloped us, womblike and kind.

"Yeah?"

"I been thinkin'," he continued.

"Yarp," I said.

"When we get older, let's build two big log houses side by side."

"Mhh hmmm," I said in my best Kermit the Frog voice.

"We'll build a bridge that joins the houses on the top floor, and there'll be no doors, okay?"

I looked at him. He was serious. Always working on plans. He was going to be an engineer. His dad had wanted to be one too, but never had the balls or the grades. I let Hank talk.

"And what we could do is, we could have visitors whenever we wanted. Day or night."

I watched him. Sometimes he had nightmares, but this was good. This was a fine plan.

"And we could have pizza parties, sleepovers, anything. Any old time. Just us."

I smiled. "Love it. Best plan ever."

I could feel the pride swell inside him. "And if we got married, our wives could move in, but they'd have to understand that what we have is more than being brothers. More than twins, even."

The night his dad walked out, his mom called my mom, and I was allowed to sleep over, even though it was a school night. We played Nintendo, and I pretended not to see the tears dripping down Hank's face.

"Go on," I said now.

"They'd have to understand that we were allowed to share them. We could go to the landslide, go skidooing, and we could all sleep together on one big bed."

Hank's cousins were gorgeous. This could be magic. "We'll have to get a king size," I reasoned.

He shrugged and smiled, proud of himself, my buddy who was so small for his age. My extra soul who had taught me how to tie my shoelaces and tell time. I put my arm around him before pushing him away. He held his pinky out. "Promise?"

I nodded and wrapped my pinky around his. "Promise."

I poured half of the Pop Rocks into my mouth before handing him the box. I gurgled all robotic-like and then opened my mouth so he could hear the ocean of science and strawberry fizz. "Seal it."

He did the same. I could smell the chemicals roaring through the orifice of his skull. "Sealed."

* * *

So, long story short, I explained all of this to Carly when she came back to the head table. She leaned in and listened. It was like the time we bought a car together and had a finance meeting after the big "We'll take it" moment. The money guy explained things as Carly and I huddled, the heat of her scalp ruminating with mine. She'd had to break things down for me, since I did not understand the terms and conditions. This time, it was the reverse.

I looked at Hank across the dance floor, and he smiled like a wish. He raised a glass. I turtled back in with my wife.

Carly, bless her, let out her deepest breath, and we huddled.

"And this is the promise you made?" she asked at the end. She had the best teeth, the sweetest breath. I couldn't wait to snuggle after.

I nodded. "Sorry, Babe. We sealed it with Pop Rocks."

My wife was used to my antics. Nine years of hilarity and foibles. She shook her head. "But he's single. You know that, right?"

I shook my head too. "I know, Babe. For now. He likes redheads, though."

She got crushes sometimes. She even told me.

I remembered lying on the carpet that day with Hank. All the times I'd tricked him. All the no-fair Academy Awards I'd won over the years.

Carly periscoped and looked at him again. I winced and prayed. My soul hiccuped.

"Jesus," she said.

My palms hummed, like they do after you've fired a gun that outclassed and outreasoned you.

"I have considered it," she said finally, squeezing my shoulders in the rented tux with the pockets that were just for show. "This simply is not going to happen."

I nodded, sighed and took it like a soldier for all of us.

I limped across the dance floor towards Hank. He raised his arms. I orangutaned Hank, and Hank do-si-doed me.

His mom was talking to my mom.

People started dinging their glasses.

He was dressed in one of his fancy engineer suits, but he was still wearing the belt I'd got him when we graduated.

"And?" he whispered.

"No dice, fuck dink," I said.

"Dammmmmn," he said. He gripped me tighter. "She thought about it, though?"

"Maybe in the next life," I said.

He held the back of my neck, wrestling stance, ape stance, brother stance, and kissed the top of my head. "You know it."

Man Babies

Oy! If you're forty-five and you're still living at home, you're a little man baby, and shame on you! You should be cutting wood and hauling water and hunting and shovelling snow for your family and Elders. That's the only reason you should be home. You should be cooking for your parents every single night.

Am I the only one who's noticed that we have an epidemic of little man babies running around? I can't be. I refuse to be. Look at all the track pant- and hoodie-wearing Bong Generation scruffians out there. Most dads look like ex-cons now. What happened?

I'll tell you a good story, but, boy, I'm mad now. As soon as I said the MB words I got mad.

Well, a friend of mine in Fort Smith—he's a wildlife officer—he met the most beautiful woman—*oh!* This was it, he said: she was the reason he'd been waiting, right? He hunts, he traps, he's a wildlife officer, right? He goes after the poachers. Anyone who wastes meat—holy man, good luck. You'll wake up with a pillow over your face at four in the morning with a shotgun pressing your nose. No, it's not that bad, but he's as tough as they come.

First time Steve saw Karen, she had just moved back to town and was out trapping with her dad. Her cheeks were flushed, she had snow frost in her hair, she was wearing beaver-lined gauntlets and had a Ski-Doo suit on. Karen's smile just blew him away, and he asked her out for coffee in front of her father, surprising them all.

"Go for it," her dad said. "Steve's a good man."

Steve blushed, he told me.

Fast-forward to five dates later. Steve is just so happy now. The wait is over. Here they're wining and dining each other, doing the grinder on the dance floor to "Love Hurts" by Nazareth at closing time at JJ's. Everything is great, right? Even when they two-step, the crowd stops to watch, hey.

Karen was up for anything, Steve said: always happy, a great cook, the perfect bush buddy, and so in touch with herself and straight-up sexy. She was all kinds of woman, I guess.

The one thing, though, was her son was still staying with Karen at her house. She called him Baby. That was her boy. Dude, if your mom's still calling you Baby at twenty-eight and you're still living at home being an Xbox champion, looking for the fire axe in *World of Warcraft*, rocking your little hockey socks and your little track pants—if you're too busy playing Nintendo to work and earn, right, we may have a situation of learned helplessness.

And that is what the government is counting on: that our warriors will remain couch potatoes. That our languages and customs will die. That we will fade out.

So, you know, everything was going good for Steve and his lady, but it was already on his radar about Baby and he said to Karen, "So, you know … when we move in together, you know, I hope Baby gets his own pl—"

"Oh yeah," she cut in. "We talked about it. Baby said he's gonna move out. He has plans."

But Steve felt a worry 'cause Karen was still paying for her son's Telus bill every month: six hundred bucks, hey! His phone bill was six hundred bucks every month. And how many times did Steve hear, "Oh, Baby needs a bit more money. Baby's Ski-Doo went through the ice. Maybe I should get him a new one."

"Didn't he have insurance?"

"He forgot to get it," I guess Karen said.

Steve felt fear curl up cold inside of him. But he bided his time, and then one day he said, "Okay, it's only three weeks until we're moving in together. How's it going with Baby?"

"Oh, Baby's got it all lined up," she said. "Everything is going okay. Don't you worry."

"Okay," Steve says.

But then I guess Karen said something else.

"Where is this coming from?" she asked Steve point-blank.

"What?"

"I'm feeling pressure from you to kick my own son out of the life I want to build with you. I really don't like this," she said.

"Sorry," Steve said. He felt himself backsliding, but he had to make his point.

"Come on," she said to him. "If we're going to move in together, we need to be honest. You're a proud Dene man. I get it. Baby never had that. You're his first positive role model. My dream is your dream: to have him learn from you, and then we'll send him on his way. Or, even better, once he's learned all he can from you, he'll get bored with coming home to us, and he'll move out all happy and fulfilled."

Steve made himself nod.

"So," Karen said to him, "what is your greatest fear with me? Be honest."

Steve was scared, but he summoned up his courage. "I, uh, I don't want to invest years of my life with someone if this isn't forever. I may have missed the window for my own kids, but I want a life partner. I want a wife. I want to be the best husband and father for a family I can be proud of."

"But?"

Shit! She was too good.

"But I can't be proud of a son who'll mooch and be in the way of my dream."

There. He'd said it. He tiptoed his eyes in her direction. She was looking down, as if struck.

"Well," she said. "I need time to think about this, because me and Baby, we're a package deal."

Maybe it's a bad deal, Steve thought, but he pushed the worry away. "What is your worst fear with me?" he asked her, even though he already knew.

"My biggest fear is you coming between me and my son," she said.

Steve could feel his blood start to boil. He didn't want to fight. "I need to go for a walk," he said.

"Okay," she said. "I'll cook supper."

Steve was putting on his boots and parka when Karen came over to him. "I crawled through my own blood once to get Baby out of his father's drunken grip. Baby had an ear infection, and he wouldn't stop crying. It was forty below outside."

Karen stood so strong in his kitchen holding herself, Steve said. "He hit me so hard I couldn't see straight for a week," she told him. "I had two black eyes. I got to Baby just in time."

"Holy shit," Steve said to her. It was all he could think of.

Karen let Steve hold her, but she did not cry. "If you don't want us, tell me now," she said to him.

"I want you to move in with me. And I want Baby to get his own place. He's welcome at our place any time."

As soon as Steve said that last line, he told me, he could feel cold air rushing into his home. But he let that be. Karen had given him a lot to think about.

He reminded himself that he would have the power to end it for the first six months. After that, they'd be common law. By then, she could go after what he had. He had to protect himself.

Steve and I, we have so many friends, too many friends, both men and women, who have aged fast and hard from choosing the wrong partner. Steve did not want to join the miserable people he saw with their deflated faces, taking the long way home because home was the last place they ever wanted to be.

Steve decided he would mark his calendar once Karen moved in. Karen and Baby would either make his life wonderful or they'd make it a misery. If it took misery for a bit with Baby for things to become wonderful with Karen again, and if marriage was on the horizon, well... "Let's just see how this goes," he said to himself.

In the meantime, Steve kept checking in, kept checking with Karen: "How's Baby doing?" "Did Baby check out those job leads I printed up for him?" "Any word?" He noticed that his house felt chilly all the time now, even when he sat closer to his wood stove.

As they'd agreed, Karen moved in the day her lease expired. Everything was going good until guess who showed up with four Glad garbage bags at 11:00 p.m. that first night?

Baby!

"Oh, you know," Karen said to Steve. "Baby's place didn't work out. I didn't have enough for his damage deposit. Can he just stay on our couch until the end of the month?"

Steve let out the biggest soul sigh. What could he say?

Because what he heard was, "Can Baby just live on your couch for the rest of your life? Can my loser face of a dink nose son eat you out of house and home? Can my Big Rhino Baby hot-knife Jamaican finger hash with your best knives every day at 4:20? Can Baby shave his pubes in your bathtub before *you* go for a bath?"

Anyways. So Baby moved in and set up his Xbox, started calling his friends over. And he started eating—and I mean face-down-in-everything eating. And he didn't clean—he didn't do dishes, didn't vacuum. Nothing. By Day Three, Steve's home had taken on a man stench of nachos and balls' sweat.

Basically, his whole place smelled like Frog Ass.

After a couple of weeks, Steve came over to my place for coffee, and he told me: "You know, I'm a patient man. I'm nice until I'm not nice anymore. So I'll say, 'Hey, Baby, do you want to go see that cinnamon bear out by the airport? You know, there's a moose swimming across the river. I got an extra quad—let's go watch.'"

But Baby would just chew his cud and watch TV and say, "Nope. I'm good," Steve complained to me.

So Steve would try again: "Hey, Baby. The northern lights are out tonight. You know, they're all red. That only happens once every twelve—"

"Nope," Baby would say. He would wipe the milk from his cereal off his chin and smear it onto Steve's couch. "I'm good."

Yeah, so everything was still kinda good with Karen, Steve said. Even though there was a man baby living on his couch, right? Even though the TV was on all night. Even though the place reeked of marijuana and Baby smoked in the bathroom. All the while Steve kept asking Karen, "What's going on? Any movement with Baby moving out?" Stuff like that. He told me that he'd listen to himself and think, *You're nagging. You're bullying.* But when was Baby moving out?

Karen would say, "He just needs a bit more time." Or "You know he's had a rough life, right?"

We've all had rough lives, Steve wanted to say, but

hard work, good schooling, dear friends, our country foods, a sweet love and a healthy family can cure most anything.

So one day, Steve told me, he caught this poacher in the South Slave. This guy had killed seventeen cow moose in one year. All the wasted meat, you wouldn't believe it, and Steve was after him. He was after him. Finally, he caught him. "This guy is gonna go to jail," he told me. "I seized his truck and his guns. We documented spent cartridges on the floor. The guy was shooting out of his truck, right? Really bad guy."

Steve thanked the Creator and gave thanks to his dad and uncles for showing him all they knew when it came to tracking. That's how he had got the bad guy. After he handed the poacher over to the RCMP, he said to himself, "I'm just going home. When I get home I'm gonna cook. I'm gonna do a chicken stir-fry in my wok. I'm gonna make apple pie right from scratch. And bannock! I'm going to make my world-famous bannock with bear grease and the best tea ever, spruce tea. Ori. Oh, it's gonna be great, you know? And I'm gonna kiss my woman all night long. I'm just going to spoil her. I'm going to celebrate. How many months have I been after this guy, and I got him. I got him!"

Steve told me he did a little jig as he walked out of the cop shop. He even recited the Classic Dene motto, "When you're good you're good."

So Steve got all the groceries and left them at the house, ready to go, before he did some errands, and then he picked Karen up from her work. They smooched it up and then headed home. As they drove, Steve was planning the evening. He was so happy. He was going to put on CKLB. It would take him an hour or so to get the rice cooked and slice and dice the veggies as he fried up the chicken. His sweetie was happy and proud of him, but just as they pulled up to Steve's house, her emergency cellphone rings. She's a counsellor for abused women, and this is the phone she has to sleep beside.

"I gotta take this," she said to him.

"Don't worry about it, Babe," Steve told her. "I'm going to go in there and I'm gonna cook for you. I'm gonna show you how it's done. There's a reason you love me, and I'm gonna remind you what it is."

So he goes into the house, and right away he smells cigarette smoke, booze, pot, and there's Baby on the couch with his Xbox. Baby looks at Steve and says, "Hey, Stevie. The store closes in about seventeen minutes. You guys better go buy something. I'm hungry."

And Steve goes, "What do you mean? I got all that stuff for the chicken stir-fry. I'm gonna cook—"

"Ate it," Baby said. "I got the munchies."

That was the moment Steve snapped. You know when northern men snap they get quiet, even quieter than when northern women get mad. So Steve told me he walked to the fridge. "I opened it up, and the food was all gone. There were dirty dishes everywhere. There were cigarette butts in my sink. There was an empty mickey in my sink. I looked over at him, and, Baby, right away, he started yelling, "Mom! Mummy! Mum! Mum! Mum! Mum!""

So I guess Steve said to him, "She can't hear you. She's in the garage taking a call, probably saving a woman's life. It's just you and me now."

"Mummy!" Baby yelled again. He grabbed his phone. "I'm gonna text her."

Steve was all business by then, I guess. He told Baby, "You can text your mom all you want, but here's the deal: you're out of here right now. You showed up with four Glad garbage bags. There are four bags right there under the sink. You're going to go live with your grandpa. You have five minutes, starting right now."

"Or?" Baby asked.

Steve made two fists and leaned in so close that his nose was almost touching Baby's. "Or you're gonna get it."

"Mummy! Mum! Mummy!" Baby started bawling.

Steve said to him, "Listen to yourself. You're twenty-eight years old and you're calling for your mom. You don't got any money. You don't cook. You don't clean. Your mother has given everything for you." Steve glanced at his watch. "Now you have three and a half minutes."

Baby looked at Steve and lowered his voice. "You really think my mom's gonna pick you over me?"

Steve says, "Well, we're gonna find out because if she picks you she's out too. We're done!"

"Take it easy!" Baby says to him.

Steve says, "No. I'm serious! Go! Right now!"

"Hmmmph!" Baby yelled. "This is bullshit!" He jumped up and grabbed four Glad garbage bags. He ran back for his Xbox. He grabbed his little Wii. He went racing down the hall and snatched his razor and toothbrush out of the bathroom, and then he stuffed his clothes into the bags. "This is bullshit!" he yelled again.

"Yes it is," Steve said and looked at his watch again. "One minute."

Baby's little chin was just trembling, I guess, and Steve got the giggles. He felt good, he said. Every once in a while, just like his uncle had told him, a good fight clears out the cholesterol, hey?

Baby took off down the road, dragging his four garbage bags. He wore his little jacket, his little track pants, little Nike high tops, right?

Steve was watching him, already feeling so much better.

But all of a sudden Baby dropped his bags and started dancing, Steve said.

Then Baby was racing across the road, back and forth. It was like something out of WWF, Steve told me. He could not believe his eyes—or ears. "You know what?" Baby yelled. "You think you're a hero, Steve. But you're really a ZERO. You hear me?"

Steve frowned. "Is that the best tell-off you got? I was using that in kindergarten. What's next? You gonna tell me you didn't go to high school, you went to school high?"

Baby stopped. "Okay, I wasn't going to do this, but I'm going to do this. You made me." Baby then pretended to sing into a pretend microphone. Baby started strutting. He puffed up his chest and he started rapping, kind of. Steve could barely make out the words but the tune was familiar. "Wait a minute," Steve said. No way. Was Baby pretending to be the lead singer of Rage Against the Machine? Was he singing "Killing in the Name" to him?

Baby didn't let up. He was jumping up and down while holding his imaginary microphone. He then started giving Steve the middle finger. Steve got the giggles. For a temper tantrum in the middle of the road, this was too much.

"Why are you laughing?" Baby yelled. "This song was written for you, Decider!!"

And Steve yell-laughed, "Decider? Are you kidding me, Baby? That's Rage Against the Machine! I was singing that in my basement in my gonchies in Grade 7, before you were even born."

Baby was stunned. He gave Steve the finger again before slipping on ice and cracking the back of his head on the road.

Steve looked over his shoulder, he told me. Any minute Karen was going to come through that door. Thankfully, Baby got up, grabbed his Glad garbage bags and continued on down the street.

Steve watched him go until he vanished. And he didn't feel bad at all. He was thinking about how good it would feel for Baby to find his own place, to set it up the way he wanted it. He was thinking about Baby buying his first truck, that first drive home from the dealership. The pride that everyone deserves to feel when they do something special. Steve noticed that Baby's cellphone was lying in the snow. He didn't feel bad about that either.

When Karen came in, she looked around. "Where's Baby? What happened?"

"Oh," Steve said to her. "It's the most amazing thing. Baby decided to live with your dad."

Karen narrowed her eyes at him. "What? My dad is really hard on Baby. He makes him cut wood and stack wood and fill the woodbox and check the nets with him twice a day."

Steve smiled at her. "Well, he said he wants to learn from the best."

Karen frowned. "I'll just call him."

"Oh no," Steve said. "That's the thing. He said he wants to do this. Hey, you know what? I'll take you out for supper. Let's go for—"

She held up her hand. "No, I want to call Baby. I need to call my son."

Steve knew Baby's phone was still lying on the road. He'd get it later. Or maybe he wouldn't. Karen tried and tried, but no answer. She was frantic, Steve said. He saw something in her that he hadn't noticed before: guilt and regret. She was trying to make up for something. That's what this was about. Karen was trying to make up for something, and Baby was milking it to the max.

Steve said, "Sweetheart, I'm asking you. There are no groceries, because they're all gone. I'm hungry. I know you are, too. Let's make this a date night. Let me take you out."

Karen finally agreed, Steve said. They went out to the restaurant. Usually, they'd be there for four hours, dancing and watching the game. This time, they lasted about fifteen minutes, because Karen said she wanted to go home. She was worried about Baby. Maybe he'd come back. She wanted to call him on their land line.

Steve knew that was it. So they went home and the snow was falling hard, hey. As soon as they got in the house, the phone started ringing, and Baby was on the other end.

Fear sweat erupted all over Steve's body. His nipples inverted. His balls sucked back in. He was in survival mode, hey?

Karen hung up and she said, "Did you kick my son out of this house?"

Steve just told her the truth. "You're goddamned right I kicked him out, because he's a little man baby! He's twenty-eight years old and he's a mooch! He eats all our food! He's smoking dope in my bathroom!"

He gave her all his reasons. Then Karen said, "He's back tonight or I'm gone."

"Well, then, I guess you're gone," Steve said to her. "'Cause you're not helping him. At twenty-eight, Baby is a man. He should be shovelling! He should be cutting wood! He should be gathering rat root! Every time that the caribou or the moose are out, he should be hunting for the Elders! He should be learning from me how to make snowshoes—right? He should be learning from me how to hunt and trap and make the best damn dry meat in the South Slave. I've given him a hundred opportunities. We're not helping him, so if you want him back, you can go too. I'm willing to risk a broken heart for the rest of my life."

"Well, hold on now," Karen said. "Let's not get too carried away."

Steve and Karen kept talking, and I guess little Baby he got tired of being bossed around by his grandpa, because after three days of it he went down to the Friendship

Centre. He filled out every application: NAIT, SAIT, Grant MacEwan, U of A, right? He filled out every application to work with Highways. Anything to get out of Grandpa's house, eh? Even the diamond mines: two weeks in, two weeks out—anything. Right? Well, he got accepted into NAIT.

So Baby showed up at Steve's house while Karen was at work, and he said, "Steve, I just came over to say goodbye."

Steve had already heard the good news, but he decided to play dumb. "Where you going?"

"Uh, well, I got accepted into NAIT in Edmonton. My grandpa is a veteran, so I got a scholarship. I'm gonna learn how to be a carpenter."

And Steve goes, "Well, that's great. Need a ride to the airport?"

And Baby goes, "No, I'm driving down with a friend."

Steve told me he saw tears in Baby's eyes.

Right away, as soon as he was gone, Karen started sending Baby money.

So, that's the first part of the story. But it was rough on Steve. He was worried he might have been wrong about Baby being alone in the city, because how far can you push a little MB before he snaps, right?

Steve said that fall he and Karen found each other again: sleeping in, movies, snuggling, cooking, hosting, visiting, cruising. Everything he had loved in her was back again. But he was worried, so he decided to do some research. He didn't want Baby to be his enemy. He wanted Baby to become a man he could be proud of. He wanted

Baby to become a provider, a protector, a nurturer. What he found out, through his research on the computer at the office and coffee sessions at the Pelican Restaurant, was that Baby's father was a professional Baby-maker who never paid a cent in alimony or maintenance. Karen told him she'd heard 75 per cent of boys who watch their moms get hit will hit their partners later on. So she and her boy had left Baby's father with just the clothes on their backs. She wanted Baby to know a home without fear, violence, belittling, intimidation.

Hearing all this, Steve thought about Baby. The way Baby hid on the couch. His silence. His quiet watching when Steve and Karen were together. Baby was a scared little boy waiting to be welcomed into the family he should have had years ago.

But, Steve said, all that information, it didn't change his position on Baby needing to blaze his own trail at twenty-eight. Too much time had passed with Baby being treated like a, well, baby.

So, come December, Baby started emailing his mom even more often. And Karen relayed to Steve, "Baby is coming back for Christmas! Ohhh!! He's got a girlfriend. He's got a happy life! My boy lost thirty pounds!"

For the next ten days, Steve said, Karen was cooking, baking, singing, getting the house clean. She was so excited.

On December 21, Baby drives all the way up to Fort Smith in his new truck. Steve came over to give me an update. He didn't say anything to Karen, but he was worried Baby would say he wasn't going back. He was worried that Baby would want to move back in. He was worried his last four months of bliss were about to come to an end.

So Baby arrived at the house, Steve told me, and holy man he looked good. Baby was trim. He had two new earrings in. Gold. He had a leather jacket. You could hear it scrunch with every move, Steve said. It sounded like a big iguana was in the house every time Baby flexed. New boots even! I saw his new truck in the driveway, and it looked good.

Karen had put up a WELCOME HOME! WE MISSED YOU! sign, I guess. Steve spent all night blowing up balloons. Gave himself asthma, almost blew a lung. He made a feast that night, and I guess everyone was there: Baby's grandpa was there, cousins were there, nieces were there, buddies were there, and, man, Baby looked good! You could smell his leather jacket fresh from The Leather Ranch in West Edmonton Mall, Steve said. A city haircut and a new little belt buckle, and Baby told everybody he was really good. He was getting B-pluses and A-minuses and the instructors were looking out for him. He'd met a beautiful Cree woman. But Steve had a feeling, he told me, that there was gonna be a showdown.

Steve did the dishes. He stayed in the kitchen, made fresh bannock, kept the coffee going, you know. Finally, at the end of the night, everyone cleared out. They were patting Steve on the back. "Man, that was good cookin'. Mahsi cho!" Even Baby's grandfather was smiling after going back for thirds.

Steve was still wondering what was going to happen,

though. When Karen went to have a shower, Baby says to him, "Steve, can I talk to you out in the backyard?"

"Sure," Steve told him. "Give me two minutes here. Just finishing up these dishes."

After Baby went outside, Steve told me, he put on a short jacket so Baby couldn't grab it, in case they got into a fight. He tucked his braids in so Baby couldn't choke him out with them. He got his big hiking boots on so he could have traction in the snow. No gloves. He kept it bare knuckles, 'cause he knew things were gonna get bloody, eh?

So Steve and Baby were out in the back, just circling each other with the northern lights snapping above them.

"Well, how are things?" Steve asked Baby.

"Things are good," Baby says.

"Oh, yeah? How are you liking the city?"

"Oh, I love it," Baby said to Steve. "I seen AC/DC, GNR. It was good. Saw Platinum Blonde at the River Cree."

"Oh yeah?" Steve said. "So, what do you wanna talk about?"

And then I guess Baby said, "Uh, well, there's a couple things. Number one I just, it's hard for me to say, but I want to say thank you."

Steve was stunned, he told me. "You want to thank me for what?"

So Baby said, "It's terrifying when you don't know what you want to do. Like my friends, we graduated from high school, and then one wants to be a doctor, one wants to be a nurse, one's gonna be an engineer, one's getting into the military, another's gonna be a dad. Everybody had all these plans except me."

"Go on," Steve said to him. He was still keeping his distance from Baby, he told me, just in case.

"Well," Baby said, "when I went down to the city, nobody knew me. Nobody looked me in the eye when I walked down the street. I was lonely. And I was scared. I mostly just stayed home and frickin' studied, because I wanted to know what people were talking about in class. And I started going for tutoring, checking in with the Elders and the counsellors. They got Elders in Residence, even. You know, I started learning some things about myself. I'm not proud of it, man. I'm twenty-eight. I'm not getting any younger. I feel like I'm catching up to the world. Plus I dropped thirty pounds."

I guess Steve just nodded, and Baby kept going.

"And I found somebody special," Baby said. "She's making me moccasins right now. Can you believe that? Hey! I need your recipe for moose dry meat. I want to make some for her before I go back."

"Oh. No problem," Steve said. "It's Back Eddy's and liquid smoke. You use an ulu to cut the meat really thin. I'll show you how to do it."

"Okay," Baby says to Steve. "So that's part one."

And here they started circling each other again in the backyard, eh? Steve was worried, and he said to Baby, "What's part two?"

"Well," Baby said, "when I was down there in the city I took boxing."

This is it! Steve thought. "Oh you did, did you?" he said to Baby.

"Yeah. I'm good. You know, in about two years from

now, I'll have my Golden Gloves status. These fists are gonna be registered as lethal weapons."

Steve smiled to keep things friendly, he told me. "Oh yeah? Good for you."

"Yeah," Baby said. "I came back here with a plan."

Steve's mouth started to water, he told me, at the prospect of a full-on fisticuff session. "What's your plan?" he said to Baby.

"I came here to knock you right out," Baby said.

So Steve said to him, "Well, let's talk about this before you stretch me out."

Baby looked like he was almost crying, Steve said. I guess Baby told Steve, "Nobody ever stood over me before and gave me five minutes to leave what I was trusting as a safe home for me and my mom. My grandpa is a good man, but he's tough and he's hard, you know. I wasn't used to working like that. And the whole time I was down there in the city, I was scared. 'Cause nobody knows you, nobody's looking out for you, nobody has time for each other down there. So, anyways, I came here to knock you out. I want to punch you right in the nose."

And I guess Steve said to him, "All right," he says, "let's make a deal."

And Baby goes, "What?"

"I could lose my job if I get an assault charge, you know?" Steve said to him. "So no matter what happens, you gotta give me your word you won't call the cops after."

He told me that Baby, his chin just started wiggling then.

"I'll even let you have the first hit," Steve told him. "I got a glass jaw. Drive me right there. Maybe you'll get lucky."

"Ahh," I guess Baby said, not so confident now.

So Steve went, "Okay, so that's the rules: no cops and you get the first hit. But I'm here to tell you," he told Baby, "bigger men than you have frickin' dropped faster than they can frickin' blink. So let's go. You better make it good, Junior."

And then I guess Baby dropped his hands. "Or we could just hug," he said to Steve.

And Steve went, "Well, you decide. I could definitely get into a fight tonight. I wouldn't mind punching the back of your head through the front of your face. What do you say? Let's chuck some knuckles!"

"No," I guess Baby said. "We're good. We're gonna hug. Hugging's good. A hug and we're good, okay? Here I go. I'm going to let you hug me."

So Baby held his arms out, Steve told me, and Steve couldn't resist. He hugged him just hard, boy, as if he were his own son.

Just then Karen came out to see what was happening and she discovered them just holding each other up, boy.

"Ah!" She smiled and walked out to join them. "There's my men."

And that was the moment, Steve told me, that they became a family.

I Am Filled with a Trembling Light

Hey. Mahsi cho. Yes and no: maybe I threw that rock through the Northern Store window. Or maybe I was just going inside to see if I could help you RCMP guys catch the guy who did it. Maybe...

I am grateful for this coffee, I'll tell you that much. Mahsi.

The reason I wanted you to tape this is I have a story the world needs to know. If they put the tube in tomorrow, well, this is my chance to have something written down forever in our name, amen. [*Laughter*]

My great-grandmother, she lived to be 105. Are you superstitious? Think about this after we're done. They say she returned to her camp a long time ago to find her entire family killed by the Chipewyan. This was before the Akaitcho/Edzo Treaty. They say that she screamed after coming upon the bodies of her husband, her daughters, her sons, her grandchildren. She saw the war party leaving in canoes. They were laughing at her, especially the

Head Man. They always left one person behind. That's
what she said. Always one person to experience the horror, spread the fear. She could tell the men in the war
party were heading to the next fishing camp. Her sister's.
My great-ehtsi raised her hand and said a prayer before
plunging her fist into the sand. She grabbed something
from the earth. When she raised her fist into the air again,
she pulled out the Head Man's bloody heart, which was
still beating.

Think about that.

Old-time power.

Inkwoh.

Let me tell you one more:

Long time ago, the Dogribs, they used to cut off your
third finger if you were a thief. I think they should have
done that to my dad for his gambling. It would have saved
our family. Dad can't help himself. After a while, nobody
would let him at their tables or into the casinos. But Benny'd take him. Benny takes anyone.

You know Benny's back, hey? Torchy, Sfen, Finch:
they're all working for him again. How you gonna stop him
once he gets going again? You think Benny just got older?
No. He got smarter. Learned some more tricks. You know
he's famous for his mean streak, right? Your team and that
undercover took him down, hey? How long is every one of
you going to last now that he's out? You bet he's got your
names. Even the Narc's. Deals have been made.

The town is already adjusting. Steve "McQueen" fled
in the night. His trailer door's still wide open. Go look.
Didn't your day just get a little easier now Steve's gone?

You know that Steve sold four of our youth dope, and now they don't get out of bed anymore. There's something wrong with them. You'll probably try and tell me that you're building a case against Steve, but this is soul murder. Those boys will never be the same. Their parents don't work anymore. They tend to their sons all day.

I seen one of those boys once. He was shuffling in his yard, walking towards the fire that was going. His hair was long. He looked dead. Dead and walking. His uncle was trying to steer him away from the fire, but the boy was determined.

How the hell long does it take to build a case? Steve's been selling dope for years.

I get mad sometimes. It's like I'm holding the terror of the world in my hands. I can feel it all. Like a beating heart.

See how delicate that little spider is? I found it. That's patience right there, what you're holding. They say in the Cree way, every bead is a prayer. Think of all the beads that went into that. Think of all the prayers.

Anyways, you probably heard: my dad lost our home in a card game. Benny won it three days after he come back. He also won Dave's cabin, that new one. Two hundred thousand dollars across the river, and it's now Benny's. That was on the second day Benny got back. You know how long Dave worked on that cabin? Years.

A few days ago, Dad came home and told me to start packing. But with this tumour on my spine, where was I to go? You know I have cancer, right? Dad turned on the TV after that and sat there the whole evening, trying to figure out how he had lost. He'd had the hand, he said. When he woke up that very morning, his left palm was itching. Itching, itching, itching. He even ran it under water. But he was so happy. For us, an itchy palm means luck, hey? His lucky ones, he calls them. His lucky ones were saying that today was the day. He was gonna win big. Pay off his losses, pay off his bills, take everyone out for Chinese. That he lost was impossible. He just sat there and cried.

Grandma was out, and he knew when she got home he'd get it. Never mind me—I'm dying. But what would happen to her? The belly-button nubs of all of her children and grandchildren are buried under the aunty trees in our yard in medicine bags beaded and sewn by my mom before she died. Where on Earth could Ehtsi go where it wouldn't kill her to have to walk by our family home every day without being able to speak to those nubs and all our memories?

So I walked over to Benny's and knocked. I seen his security camera outside. I waved once and then waited. He always makes me wait. I knocked again. The door opened and it was Torchy. He looked at me, the state of me. Shook his head. Spit past me. Looked back at Benny sitting in his spot at the table. Always in his spot. Sits there for cards, food, meetings, scheming. The TV was on. Benny was mopping up yolk with his toast.

"And?" Torchy asked me.

"Benny," I said. "Please."

Torchy shook his head. "Sorry about your dad."

I felt my eyes pulse. "Me too."

Benny stood slowly, holding his side. White wife beater.

Gold chains. Skinnier than when he went in. Faded tattoos: a snake, a woman dancing with a dagger behind her, syllabics—Cree, Inuit. He shimmied around his table. When you play cards, you gotta sit at the table. Everyone has their spot. All these pillows. Fancy. He slowly made his way. I heard laughter in the kitchen. Maybe they were day-drinking.

"Stay outside," he said as he watched something on the TV. "I don't want death in the house."

As he came closer, I caught a whiff: the house smelled like fresh bannock and hangover soup. Then I caught a whiff of me: a hot, bloating sweet stench of mange bubbling up through my clothes. I wouldn't want me in the house either.

Long time ago, we had a warrior class. They weren't allowed to mix with other people. They walked alongside the people. They trained all the time. They were giants. Watched from birth. Taken when their voices started to change and taught to protect. You ever think about Torchy, Sfen, Flinch—why they never had women? You ever think about that? Flinch is a giant. Big boy. They say he was still growing at twenty-four. And Crow. The miracles she's performed. For her to shack up with Benny, well, that says it all. She knows a lot. You ever figure out where Benny came from? I think he has medicine. Maybe from when Snowbird and him fought. Who knows?

"Sorry about your dad," Benny said to me. As I mentioned, he's skinny now. Some men put on weight when they go to the pokey. Benny looks weak, dusty. Someone said he got stabbed on his last day inside. I can believe it.

I stared at him. "Me too."

"You knew this was coming," he said.

It was the way he said it that bothered me. A finality to it. A condemnation.

"Yeah," I said, just to speak.

"You have three days to vacate your home," he said, eying me. "Starting yesterday."

I let out my breath. There is nowhere I want to move to. I stood there thinking that. I was going to die in the hospital. I wanted to. "Bring on the morphine," I said to myself. "When they put that tube in, give me the city drugs." I was looking forward to floating away.

"What about my grandma?" I asked him.

"I told him how many times to walk away," Benny said. "He didn't listen. He had his chance."

"He never listens." I shrugged. I thought of my father's eyes, red-rimmed from crying. Hating himself for being so weak.

"What can I do to change this?" I asked Benny, looking up at him. "A dying man is asking you. Our house is falling apart. It ain't going anywhere. How about take it after me and Ehtsi are gone?"

As he thought about it, a burst of laughter came from the kitchen. He glanced back and smiled before remembering that death was standing on his doorstep. I noticed that scar over his eye. The one Snowbird gave him.

"Okay, son," he said. "You're a good boy. I've never had to worry about you. When was the last time you went to the city?"

I considered it. "Years."

He ran his hand along his side. "Feel like catching the 5:00 p.m. flight?"

How else could I reply?

"Okay," I said. "What do I have to do?"

And that's how, six hours later, I ended up at the casino in Edmonton standing with a near-blind Cree medicine woman in the parking lot.

Her sons were with her. Crees, I think, and maybe Nakota? The taxi took me right there.

The sky is so big in Edmonton. I could hear the train far off. I loved the city lights. It was so long since I been to the city. It was stinky. Loud. I should have been hungry, but I don't eat much now. I have a feeling anything I eat feeds the tumour. Shit, I'm going to die soon. I never even seen the world. But I had to save our home. For Grandma. My ehtsi. She never gives up on anyone.

Before I left, Benny gave me a thousand dollars cash. Told me to help the old woman. Because I was already gone, he said, I could help. His instructions were simple: "The old woman's sons have turned Baptist, except one. That one owes me. Big time. If you do this for me in my name, you get your house back. Got it?"

"Yes, Benny. Mahsi."

I've always loved that sign he has at his place up high in neon colours: BENNY'S WHOLESALE: BECAUSE IT'S ALL ABOUT COLLATERAL. You ever just sit in the dark and think about that? He's telling the whole wide world what makes him tick. He's got that other sign, NOBODY LOVES A DRUNKEN INDIAN, hanging up in his warehouse. He's a racist who also sees opportunities. He came up here and saw how lost we were and decided to profit off it. Look at the thousands he's made bootlegging. No drugs. He doesn't like drugs. Any of his men use drugs, they're out. I heard he lost a brother to drugs. Maybe it was a son. Or he's got a brother on the street, maybe. But he's got a hate-on for drugs.

They say Crow turned him when the two of them got together. Her sweet whispers, I guess. He turned protector. Sure, his boys run booze. They have to, to make soonyows, but they set this town straight. They do more than all of you. You all rotate out the first chance you get. It's just about biding your time. But think about what Benny's boys did to Lester. Didn't Lester show up here at the cop shop holding his ears in his hands, begging to confess? Didn't he admit he was using drugs to get young girls?

People talk. You ever watch Crow tan moosehide? She can go all day. Chews snuff. Red Man. She's old school. You think she doesn't know your name?

Oh, yeah: back to the casino.

Benny had told me they'd be waiting for me in a van in the casino parking lot.

As the cab pulled away, I folded my receipt in my right pocket with the change. You could not miss this van of Indians. An airbrushed white wolf charged along one side of the van. It was running under a full moon. It looked angry. There was a big cross of sweetgrass hanging from the rear-view mirror.

The passenger and driver doors were open to welcome the breeze. Two Indians sat in the front. One was handsome. Marlon Brando handsome. The other looked rugged. Marlon Brando was reading something on his phone. The rugged one watched me. They were both in their thirties, maybe. They sat up as I got closer. They could see what the tumour had done to my spine, how it was like walking with tightening ropes. How I had to twist my neck for balance.

The old woman had a walker. She was standing by the vehicle. Her hair was long. It looked like she was wearing two dresses, one over top of the other. I loved her bracelets. Her earrings. Her blue runners. The way she held her face up to the last heat of the sun. Tiny eyes. Looked like tree sap was holding her eyelids shut.

I walked towards the van and raised my hand.

"Here for Benny?" the rugged one asked.

Marlon Brando returned to reading his phone.

I had to tilt my head up to see them both. "Yes, sir," I said. I should have polished my shoes. I must have looked like a dusty monster all humped up.

I stretched my hand out to shake theirs. The rugged one's hand was rough. Marlon Brando's grip was light as he leaned over his brother.

"Our mom." The rugged one pointed with his lips. "Violet."

"Hello, Aunty," I said.

The old woman extended her hand, and I took it gently. "I'm here to help," I said.

"I know'd it," she said. She spoke Cree to me next, a prayer. I felt it wash over me. I noticed one of her eyelids, how it opened slightly. She could see a little bit. She could see me. I couldn't tell you how rough I looked. I stopped looking in mirrors a long time ago.

That's when the limo came up to us, like a wolverine. Slow. Quiet. Ready.

The driver was the biggest Cree in the world. He gave us all a look before buttoning his suit jacket and opening the back door. Out stepped a grasshopper of a young man. Nice suit. Nice shoes. Big brown hook of a nose. Long braids. "Hello!" the young man said. "Tansi!" He walked around shaking everyone's hands. He took Aunty's hand in both of his to greet her.

"Good evening, everyone. Thank you for coming. Tansi, Aunty." The man spoke Cree to her and she answered that way. He laughed and clapped his hands. They'd met before. "Which of you is Simon?" he called.

I raised my hand.

"I'm Randy. I just got off the phone with Benny, and we agree to his terms."

I nodded. Who knows where Benny's reach ends?

"Anyone who isn't here to help from here on in," the man named Randy announced, "please be our guest at the buffet. We'll only be an hour. I'm happy to call one of you when we're done. Phil, take their number."

The rugged one had started smiling when the free supper was offered. But Marlon Brando put his phone away with a look of fear as Phil approached him. When Phil reached for his phone in his inside pocket, that's when I seen his gun. Shoulder holster. Holy shit. This was full throttle. Phil held up his phone, read out a number. Marlon Brando nodded. They were not strangers.

"Okay," Randy said. "Are we good?"

Phil the driver nodded, and the woman's sons stepped out of the van. They were dressed in a uniform of sorts: braids, wife beaters, long shorts, high white socks, black runners. They shut the van doors, hugged their mom gently.

"Thanks, Mom," Marlon Brando said softly. The old woman nodded and looked down. He kissed the top of her head before joining his brother.

So there we were: a Cree Elder and me next to a stretch limo in a casino parking lot with a giant Cree and a shiny Cree.

"Are you ... well?" Randy asked me.

"No," I said.

"Sorry to hear it," he said. He wiped his hand on his pant leg. "Benny never told me."

"It's okay," I said. "What do we have to do?"

"Aunty?" Randy said.

The old woman was sitting down by now. She had a doohickey on her walker you could lock so it wouldn't roll away on you, which meant you could use it as a chair too. My grandma would like that. Maybe the Northern could bring one of those walkers in for her, or the Health Centre.

"Mah," she said. It was like her soul was sniffing out a beast in the building.

Randy looked around to make sure no one could hear him. "We have a family using Indian medicine to steal money from our high-paying VLTs." He ran his hand over his chin. "Aunty, I need you to tell us which of the machines they've doctored. If you can take this bad medicine away, your family's debt to Benny is paid."

Debt? I wondered at that.

"Simon?" He looked at me. "You help Aunty in whatever way she wants, and you get to keep your family's house."

A little spot in the bottom of my heart, the only part the sickness hadn't spun its web into, lit with hope. I could smell sweetgrass on the old woman. She'd smudged before she came here.

Randy let out his breath, and I could see beads of sweat on his forehead. "Aunty, what can we do to make this happen?

The old woman thought about it for a minute. "The people," she said. "They can't be there."

"Already arranged," Randy said. "We told our casino customers there was a water leak, so it's all cordoned off with yellow tape."

The woman thought some more. "I can't go deep into the casino, me. Medicines can't mix. This one here"—she used her chin to point at me, and I seen a sparkle where her open eye was—"can lift me just one step inside."

"No problem," I said. I may be hunched over, but I'm still strong.

Phil folded up Aunty's walker and put it in the trunk as we got her settled into the limo. I sat across from her. I could see leather woven into her braids. The car engine was so quiet. It was almost peaceful.

I was disposable. That's why I was there. If anything medicine touches you, you're done, but I was done anyway. This was Benny's strategy. Even I could see it.

"They are going to kill my son," the old woman whispered to me, "if I don't do this."

I tapped her hand gently. "Okay, Aunty. I'm here to help you. Anything you need. You can trust me."

We pulled up parallel to the side of the casino. Crazy close. The doors opened from the inside. I saw cameras recording us.

We got out, and I steadied the walker for her. You could hear the ding ding ding of the machines inside, and right away we were covered in cigarette smoke.

"Cold," she said to me as soon as she stood. "Can you feel it?"

I couldn't. The sun was still out. I could feel the heat from the parking lot.

"Lift me," she said.

She held her arms out. I stepped behind her and lifted her one step into the casino, propping her up from behind.

And that's when I seen a slice of Hell.

So many people pacing back and forth, shuffling to and fro. All them suffering because they couldn't get to those VLT machines. I've seen the way my dad's spirit is pulled from the house when the phone rings and he hears there's a game in town and someone's calling him to come down and lose. I felt that feeling pass through me one time. I was walking down the hall beside our kitchen, and it roared through me. Just cold, boy. And I could feel it now.

The sign in the casino parking lot showed some white guy throwing dice with a blonde, a brunette, a redhead hanging off his shoulder. Everyone had white teeth.

Everyone was happy. What I saw in that casino was fat, dying people drowning in their bodies, some still wearing their pyjamas. Indians. Asians. Not a lot of whites. It was like a plane had exploded and these were the bodies thirty thousand feet in the air.

They were huddled behind the yellow tape. Some had settled for smaller VLTs. Others were restless, shifting from foot to foot. No one looked at us. Not a soul. It was like we weren't even there. That's when I felt something charge through Aunty. I was holding onto light somehow.

She raised her head from praying and pointed at one machine. "That one."

I was amazed. How could she sense anything through the noise? Through the darkness? Randy stepped around us, careful not to touch her or me. He snapped his fingers, and a Cree man wearing overalls ducked behind the VLT and started strapping it up to a dolly.

Aunty shivered. "I'm freezing," she said. "Tell him to not touch what he finds with his bare hands. He should not touch it. It will be in the middle of the machine."

"I'll tell him," Randy said.

She looked at me. "Take me out," she said. "We are done."

I made sure Aunty was secure in the limo. Phil, the driver, waited outside for Randy.

"Where are you from?" Aunty asked me.

"Fort Simmer."

"I was there once," she said. "My dad used to travel up there to help the people. You have pelicans."

I smiled. "Yes, we have—"

She reached out and wrapped her hands gently around my neck. I froze. Her hands were burning.

"I'm sorry," she said.

She was talking about my life. "Me too. I've never even smoked. My dad does. Maybe it's from that. My mom died of cancer too."

She kept her hands there for a bit before letting me go. She folded her arms over her tummy, like she was hugging herself. "Your grandma will be proud of what you did."

"What did I do?"

She cocked her head to the left, to listen to something. Then she nodded. "It's what's coming, they told me."

"Who?" I asked.

But she looked down.

Randy leaned into the limo then, wiping his hands with a wet rag. "Aunty, thank you so much. Our worker is going to take the machine apart. Wearing gloves, as per your instructions. While he's doing that, I'd like for you two to go eat. On us, of course. When he's done, I'll come back and get you."

"I can't eat in there," Aunty said. "Can you take us somewhere else?"

"Sure," he said. "There's a Denny's nearby."

So that's where we went. We ordered breakfast at night, the two of us. An omelette for me. Lots of cheese and ham and onions and peppers. Raisin toast. Suddenly, I was starving. So was Aunty. We went to town. I don't even remember if we talked at first. The coffee was fresh and hot. Oh my goodness, it was heaven. Phil, Randy's driver, stayed out in the parking lot. Did he have kids, I wondered? How many hours at a stretch did he work?

"You are a good boy," Aunty said to me as she sipped her coffee.

"Thank you," I said. "Mahsi."

"You'll be with your mom again soon. Is there something you'd like to do before you pass?"

I thought about it. I couldn't save my dad. I had tried for years. I was really gonna miss my ehtsi. Her laugh. Cooking for her. But maybe there was something useful I could do before I was gone.

Aunty and I talked for a bit about things. She told me about Heaven. What it's like. She had visited once in her sleep and seen the other side. She gave me light in my bones with what she told me, but I'm not going to talk about it here on tape.

After we ate, Phil drove us down under the casino. There was a bakery, a dentist, a doctor, even a jail, kind of. They had everything under that casino so you never had to leave. We drove to the service garage where the VLT had been taken apart. The guy doing it had laid out tarps for each section. Randy was waiting for us there too. He sent the worker outside for a smoke.

"These VLTs are assembled in different parts of the world," Randy explained, "so that the Mafia can't get control of them through our workers. Each of our VLTs is shockproof, tamper-proof. You name it."

He was sweating. I wasn't sure why.

"My question is," he said as he pointed with his chin, "how did they get that into one of our machines? It was in the centre."

We looked over towards the workbench, and there it was: the spider you're holding now, made out of black glass beads.

"They could put that in your beating heart while you're talking to me," Aunty said. "Distance is nothing to them."

Randy dry-swallowed. We all heard it. "But how?"

"This power," Aunty said, "is also the power that could cure just about everything. It's the same. And that's what's so sad. They could be saving lives."

"Will it stop now if we bury it?" Randy asked her.

"Yes. And then we need to smudge."

So we did exactly that. We smudged. After that Aunty asked me to bury the spider. The earth would take it, Aunty said. The spider was in a brown paper bag, and I put on gloves before handling it. As Aunty and I went to bury it, I held the bag all the way there.

In the time it took me to dig a huge hole in a field behind the casino, with Aunty's head bowed and her praying on her walker, a new treaty was made. I dug and dug and dug. Maybe it was during the car ride that I thought of it. Maybe it was when I knelt to bury the bag. Maybe when I reached into the heart of the Earth a cold hand was waiting and held mine and a voice whispered to me. Maybe I slipped this little black spider into my jacket when Randy and Phil were on their phones with their backs to us reporting to their bosses.

All that's in that hole in the earth is a little brown paper bag with tobacco gently sprinkled on top of it.

See: I made a deal.

The spider spoke to me in cold little whispers: *Give it to him give us to him give us give us give us give us to him.*

I could feel something gathering like a roaring wind, something cold pulling its tendrils out from under my skin. I felt it unbraid itself from around my bones and sinew. I felt it untickle my brain stem like a black octopus uncoiling, realizing I was the wrong meat. I felt the unleeching of it all that night, once I was home in my own bed. After a while, I felt that roar of the wind pass through my fingers into this spider of glass, and now I've given it to you.

It wanted me to bring it to you so it could take you.

With it comes my tumour.

I'm cured, see?

I worked at the Friendship Centre before I got sick, as a janitor. Maybe you saw me there. They were still paying me, even though I mostly didn't show up anymore. The smell from the cleaners made my dizzy. I had to lie down on the couch in the foyer the last time I was there. They called a cab for me. Garth didn't even ask for money. He saw the mass on my neck. "Jesus, Simon," he said. "Holy shit."

It was through my listening as I pushed the mop around that I learned something horrible about this town. A lot of kids had started to come in to talk to our counsellor, and I heard them talking in the halls. Little Crees, Chipewyans and Dogribs. All Native kids who came in scared. No parents. None of them had parents. That was the clue. That was the key.

All those little kids you been touching at boxing class

when they're working out. All the times you helped them change.

What you're holding now is for them and the terror you brought their way.

You're going to die cold and alone with a tube down your throat.

Me? My family, we will continue.

You don't remember this, but when I was little, my family lived in Rae. Behchoko. You were just starting out there. Already feeding your hunger.

You don't remember what you did to me, but I do. It all came back to me when I heard those kids talking at the Friendship Centre.

I'm one of probably a hundred kids you murdered inside.

This spider you hold now is our kiss back to you.

As the tumour takes hold and your face twists, think of every young boy you ever stole. We've all been shuffling towards the fire because of you.

Like my dad, you can't stop yourself. They should have taken off all of your fingers when you were in Rae so you could never grab a boy again.

We have a long memory in the North.

So I confess: I did throw that rock through the window of the Northern. I'll pay Reggie at the store for it when I'm out. Lock me up if you want. It is an honour and a privilege to be in the same place where Snowbird once turned himself to smoke and slipped out through the keyholes.

You think you know us?

You don't.

You never did.

All you saw up here were victims and dirty little Indians.

But we bide our time.

Like our ancestors.

Start praying. You probably should. See if it helps.

Oh. One more thing. In that Denny's, after Aunty told me what Heaven is like, she said to me, "That man who sent you here."

"Benny?"

"Look where he sits. Under the pillow. There's an ace of spades taped upside down where he can reach it."

That's how he won our house. That's how he won that cabin. He's still cheating.

Before I threw that rock, I told Dad about this, and I told Dave. They're over at Benny's right now. Torchy, Sfen, Crow, Flinch: they're tough, but they're outnumbered. Dave's related to half the town.

Don't be surprised when the ambulances start rolling out.

Don't be surprised when Benny phones for help.

This is gonna be fun, seeing how it all turns out.

One more day. When you come as close to dying as I did, one thing you learn is that in the end we all wish—we all beg—for one more day.

I have mine now in spades, and I am filled with a trembling light. The trembling light of my ancestors. The trembling light of all the time now I have left.

Oh. There's the sirens.

I want to lie down in that cell and plan the rest of my life and listen to what happens next.

Now take me away.

Good night.

[*Audio file ends*]

Ehtsèe/Grandpa

The time I showed my ehtsèe the movie *E.T.*, it was years ago. He was in on his own from Behchoko, getting a check-up. My grandmother was ... well, they had had a disagreement.

It was summer. My mom's house was quiet, peaceful. She'd worked hard to rebuild her life after she and her boyfriend separated. There were rumours Patrick was having an affair. He denied it up and down, but Mom had "the sense." So she decided to take a job in Yellowknife, eight hours north from Fort Smith. The idea was for Patrick and her to take some time to think about what was going to happen next. Patrick and I had gotten along great for the past nine years. I just couldn't imagine him cheating. The situation was so unbelievable that I wasn't sure what to do. But I did know my mom needed help around the new house she was renting. It was weird, because our family had built a log home when we were all together. My question was, why did Patrick get to stay in our family's log house, which my father had built with his bare hands? All of this was why I'd chosen Yellowknife for the summer as a part-time student researcher with the Dene National Office: to help my mom and be closer to my grandparents. Ehtsı̨ and Ehtsèe lived an hour and thirty-five minutes down the road in Fort Rae. "Behchoko," as they were calling it now, or perhaps as it had always been named.

I was watching *Oprah* after spending the day raking, bagging leaves and tidying up my mom's yard. I'd had a toke and was feeling buzzed. There was a knock on the door. I went around the corner and there, through the curtains, was the perfect silhouette of my grandfather puffing his little pipe: Ehtsèe. Said with breath. Said with respect. Ehtsèe: the miracle worker. The medicine man. The chanter. The holy man.

Grandpa was looking away, as if listening to something. I ran back, grabbed my camera, snuck up on the perfect portrait and took it. I answered the door after putting my camera down. It will always be the greatest picture of our lifetime together.

Tłı̨chǫ. He spoke what they used to call us: Dogrib. He said my mother's name and I told him she was at work, that she'd be home soon.

He stood there, looking away. He folded his hands around his pipe before sliding it into his jacket pocket. I never saw him light that pipe. Not once. He just liked the taste of it, I guess. It was made of either clay or red willow. I never saw it close up. It was rumoured that was where he kept his medicine power.

"Leedee Na Woo Nee?" I asked him. Would you like some tea?

"Heh eh," he said and came in. It took him forever

to take off his moccasin rubbers, and I could smell bush smoke on him.

"Nezi?" I asked him. "Are you good?"

"Heh eh," he said. "Good," he said in English.

We were from worlds apart, yet his blood flowed through mine. I was proud to be his grandson. He looked so small without my ehtsı. How I remember the difference in the words is, with Ehtsı for grandma, I always think the final *ee* sound is stronger than the final *eh* sound in Ehtsèe. Just like owls and ravens: the female is always stronger, bigger. That's how my grandparents were. My grandmother was cheeky, tough, firm. Yet she cried when we arrived for a visit and she cried when we were leaving. She'd kiss our hands and bow, kiss our hands and bow, kiss our hands.

I motioned for my grandfather to have a seat in the living room, said that I would call my mom. Maybe her boss would let her leave early. I put the water on to boil.

My grandfather sat in my mom's living room on the big couch and looked up at all the photos: my sister, my dad. So many pictures of my mom with Patrick, her hope for them as a couple all over the room. It was like she was manifesting their happiness. And there were pictures of Grandpa, Ehtsı, them together, our uncles. All the art. All the plants. The books. The TV. I tried calling my mom's office, but she had moved to another department and no one could find her number. It was lame.

I had rented *E.T.* the night before from the Yellowknife library, my favourite place on Earth along with the loft my father had built for me in the log house. I wanted to watch the movie again and see if it had stood the test of time.

After a minute, I hit "play" and it started. I motioned to my grandfather that a good movie was coming on. He crossed his legs, squinted and sat back to watch the film that had changed my life forever. He watched intently, but he kept looking right. It was as if he'd forgotten that my grandmother wasn't there beside him.

I decided to make toast and butter and jam for my grandfather. We had no dry meat left. My mom and I were mooches who showed up in Behchoko and usually took a big brown bag of it home. As I prepared his tea, I thought of him in the next room. He'd lost his entire family decades ago and as a young boy—an orphan—made his way through the Mackenzie Mountains to be with the Tłı̨chǫ. The Dogrib. He was a Mountain Dene. He and his dog found the way together, and when they got to Tłı̨chǫ territory, they were met by guards. TB and influenza were killing many Dene. My ehtsèe was not welcome at first. But he explained where he was from, and they asked him how long it had taken him to travel there. He told them, and the guards looked at each other. They did not believe that you could make it through to the Barren Lands in that short a time.

"I will show you," Ehtsèe told them. "Me and my dog."

And he did. The route shaved off two extra days of travel for the Tłı̨chǫ, and that is why we have our family name: Sih. It means mountain. I had also heard that my grandfather performed many miracles when he was young. He took a hunter's appendix out with his knife. He cured a stutterer. He tied a man's mouth shut over a distance, a man who was spreading lies about us as a family.

And now here we were. Together. Watching *E.T.* From time to time, he would point to the TV, and I could tell he wanted to ask me questions. I did my best to answer using sign language. As happy as I was, I felt that old soul ache of not being fluent in Tłįchǫ. I had about eighty words in me, but I wasn't conversational. Being fluent was my dream. It was always my dream. I was so worried about our language, but I was raised away from the Tłįchǫ, and we never spoke it at home.

Grandpa cried when he thought *E.T.* was going to die. I cried too. We took turns blowing our noses into Kleenex. I kept the movie running so we could each maintain our dignity.

At the end, my grandfather was so happy. When the credits came on, he gave me a thumbs-up and smiled. "Nezi!" he said. I helped him into the bathroom and then I helped him out onto our porch and settled him in a chair. He tasted his pipe as I made him more tea. I asked him if he was hungry. He wrinkled his nose and shook his head.

"Good movie," he said. "Good boy. Good friend."

I almost started crying again.

He tried asking me questions about my life, but I didn't know if I answered correctly. He nodded, watching me, watching me, watching me. My grandpa. I showed him my portraits of Elders from different Nations, all the children too. I carry my portfolio around for clients. For him to see the button blankets, the Sun Dance Makers, the Matriarchs, the braids, the beautiful brown skin, the veterans, the pride. He patted my shoulder and nodded. "Nezi," he said. "Nezi."

I told him that I was working on my master's at UBC and that the people there were strong. The Musqueam. I told him I helped out a lot with ceremonies on campus. Sweat lodges. I said I was getting ready to go into the lodge when I returned. I saw him stop nodding, and he looked at me in a new way.

My mom came home, and soon after that my uncles showed up. They drove my ehtsèe the hour and thirty-five minutes that it takes to return to Behchoko.

That night, my mother woke me up to say that Grandma was on the phone. She had a message for me from Grandpa, which my mom translated.

"Grandpa says you are not to go into the sweat lodge, because that is not our way. That medicine is from the south. When you go in, they wrap a blanket around you. The more times you go in, the more blankets. If Grandpa ever has to work on you—even from the other side—he will have to take off those blankets, and he could lose time. He could lose you trying to take those blankets off, Grandson."

I nodded as my mom passed on my grandma's message. I listened and understood.

"You can help," my grandma relayed through my mom. "Help them with the fire, the water, but you must not go in. You are our grandson. Will you listen?"

I nodded.

"Say it," my mom said.

"I will not go in," I said.

She and her mom spoke Tłıchǫ, and then my mom hung up.

"How come my dad told her you showed him a movie about a mushroom who helped a boy?" she asked me.

"A mushroom?" I said.

"Yes," she said. She looked very serious.

I started laughing. "It was *E.T.*"

"What?" she said. "Why did you show him that movie?"

"Because you never gave me your new work number, you," I said. "I had no choice."

Then she started laughing too.

"Know how to say mushroom in Tłchǫ?" she asked. "Dlòodìi. It means squirrel food or frog house."

I could have asked why she had never taught my sister and me Tłchǫ but I didn't. I knew that we had been raised in Smith because of the drinking and violence and chaos in Behchoko. In Smith we were raised with the Cree, the Chipewyan, the French, the Gwich'in, the Inuit, the Slavey and other friends from across Canada. We had a happy upbringing. We built our own log house as a family. I think that was our proudest achievement. Well, and we partied tamely. We were proud of that too.

I was happy for a long time after that, because I felt like my grandfather had heard me. He'd understood. I was happy he thought of *E.T.* when he thought of me. I was so proud I'd shown him the portraits I was taking.

Even so, to my shame, I did not see him or my ehtsı̨ again that summer. I was caught up with work in the small capital city of Yellowknife, the cookouts in Mom's back-yard, my weed.

My uncles were always in competition to help Grandpa, because it was rumoured that my ehtsèe was going to choose soon who to pass his medicine onto when he crossed over. The only problem was that my uncles drank. Hard. One by one they were losing their families, by getting kicked out. One or another would show up at Mom's door at four in the morning asking for money and a coffee. Sometimes my mom let them in; sometimes we waited them out.

* * *

As time went on, I got interested in becoming an archivist. I would devote my life to archiving and helping the people, I decided. I would be able to share recordings from Elders I had interviewed years or decades before. I kept taking portraits, and I started selling my services. I'd move into a community for a month or two and archive, photograph, interview community members, leaders and Elders. I loved it. I was positive that this was why I was born.

When the invitation came for me to be the Tłı̨chǫ Archivist in Residence, I jumped at the chance. I was in a disastrous relationship at the time. Abusive. Holy cow, Harmony just dragged me right out. I had little left of myself, but this was my chance. Harmony helped me pack, and I think we both knew I was never coming back. My stories had no power with her or her family or her friends. No one had time for them. I could tell she didn't believe half of what I shared with her about the North, my family, what I was hoping could be ours. By the time I left I was soul sick.

I felt my old self returning with every mile I gained on my return to Yellowknife. I had a week there before my two months in Behchoko. My mom was overjoyed that I was free. She'd seen me vanish in that relationship with Harmony, had heard it in my voice when she called.

Now that I was in my mom's new home, I relaxed into her couch, her cooking, her laughter. The North was going to cure me. My clothes didn't fit me anymore. I didn't fit in the world. I'd always enjoyed my pot, but over time I'd become a gentle slave to it. I knew exactly how many days I had left in my stash, how many joints, how many puffs, how many, how many, how many. When I first got high as a teenager, my tongue used to tingle. I used to wait for that, hope for it, ride it out, let it take its time. Now my tongue just felt fat. Explain that, someone. The tingle was gone, and I missed it.

When I moved to Behchoko, I had a mild panic attack. Where would I buy my weed when I ran out? It was such a small town, and I didn't want anyone to know I puffed. I detested the idea of going to Yellowknife to score when all I wanted was to stay still and breathe in as much Tłįcho everything as I could. My time there was my chance to become conversational, and I did my best.

"Zhah" for snow. "Gocho" for ancestors. "Adu!" for "I'm scared." Baby steps.

The work was pretty simple. I lived in a teacher's house, fully furnished—she was down south on maternity leave—and I interviewed Elders and took portraits of the kids and Elders and teachers. At night, I would upload the portraits, along with each person's signed permission, and transcribe the interviews I'd done. Holy cow, it was fun. I learned a lot. I learned about protocol for handling caribou bones and hide; I learned about the Chipewyan/ Dogrib war and how the leaders Akaitcho and Edzo had made peace together at Marion Lake. I recorded stories like "How Frog Brought Winter for Everyone," "The Time the Blue Jay and Whisky Jack Traded Wives," and a heart-breaking story about why we need to listen to our parents when they tell us to work or move quickly. I had no idea we believed in reincarnation. I learned from other Elders about a game that my grandfather used to play, where he dressed up in a mask and chased people. It was a cere-mony I wrote down called Dzèhkw'įį. The ceremony was so scary the priest had tried to forbid it, but the people continued the game in secret. My grandfather and grand-mother were out on the land when I started my term in Behchoko, at Stagg River. I couldn't wait to see them, to record them, to take their portraits, to share time.

Most of the junior Elders I photographed would ask me the same question: "Has your grandpa decided yet who gets his medicine?"

I thought it curious. Most elder Elders didn't ask me that. It was the younger generation who did.

I'd shrug. "Oh, I'm not too sure."

I did hear rumours about my uncles arguing over who had been the best son. Yet, and I hate to say it, these were the same uncles I'd see drinking, stumbling on wobbly legs at 6:00 a.m., either in Behchoko or out on the streets in Yellowknife. Booze was eating my family alive. That's why I didn't drink. I never had.

One thing I learned in community discussions, and a thing that worried me, was that the Bathurst caribou numbers had dwindled from hundreds of thousands to only nineteen thousand. We were down to a system where we hunted with tags. The majority of northern leaders agreed this was the best way to manage the herd. Yet there was still poaching and, worse, the wasting of meat by our own people. I had heard a long time earlier that the Cree say when you break a treaty with the animals, like you make them suffer or you waste the gift of them, what comes doesn't come for you, it comes for your children.

As the weeks passed, I could see my payments were not coming from the Band. At first I thought maybe there was a hold on payment, but after three weeks my Visa was maxed out and I was running low on my weed supply. I had thirty-six dollars in my wallet. That was it. This was me. And when I didn't have my three daily puffs I got achy, snappy, dazed.

"Eff this," I thought one morning, after I'd been checking my bank account, oh, a hundred times a day. "If they're not going to pay me, I'm taking the rest of the day off." I decided to make a run to Yellowknife.

And who did I see on the highway waiting for me outside of Behchoko?

My grandparents.

Oh dear, I thought. As happy as I was to see them, I had heard stories from my uncles about the scenarios they were capable of in terms of their Elderly demands. I knew that if I picked them up, it would be Bingo, Walmart, KFC, more Bingo, church, A&W, back to Bingo, possibly paying for them at the Super 8 for a night, plus bags and bags of groceries that I'd have to pay for. Along with meals out all day, all weekend. My mom was visiting friends in Fort Providence, and she had both her house keys.

I had no money. I was going through withdrawal. A headache was starting to split my head wide open, and I needed a puff of the good stuff.

They flagged me down. My grandmother was waving her arms around like windmills, but when my grandpa waved his hand waist-high, well, how could I say no? He never asked me for anything. I had a soft spot. Maybe he could take away my headache.

I pulled over.

As they got in, my grandmother climbed right in the back and fell asleep. Her luggage was a plastic Northern bag with a change of clothes in it, or maybe it was knitting and a pillow. I could smell the heavenly scent of fresh tanned moosehide. My grandfather wasn't carrying anything except his little pipe, which he put in his front pocket before getting settled. Maybe this was only a day trip. A quick trip. He looked at me, shook my hand, smiled and then fell asleep himself. I decided to drive and make the most of this.

As we headed toward Yellowknife, I remembered that I had hidden a joint on the inside panel of the truck on the driver's side, behind some paperwork. I reached in and found it. *Yes!* I waited another twenty minutes, slowed down, lowered my window and decided to light up. It was 4:20 somewhere.

Long story short?

My grandfather asked in Tłįchǫ: "What smells like dirty socks?"

I told him it was cigarettes from the US.

He told me to let him try. He was going to show me.

To this day, I do not know what overcame me. I've always had a problem with sharing. Ask my sister. She'll tell you. I told Grandpa that he had to hold the smoke in his lungs. He did exactly that. And then he coughed, coughed, coughed, which woke my grandmother up. She told us both we didn't know what we were doing. She was going to show us. My grandfather explained that these were the smokes that John Wayne used to smoke and that you had to hold the smoke in, which she did before she coughed, coughed, coughed.

All of this and no water in the vehicle.

So we took turns hotboxing in my truck, and then we ended up entering the city. By the airport.

"I'm hungry," my ehtsı̨ said.

"Heh eh," Grandpa said. "Me too."

They both looked straight ahead.

"KFC?" my grandmother asked.

I nodded. I could afford KFC for all of us.

The crazy thing, though, was when we arrived my grandmother got the giggles. Then my grandfather got the giggles. Then I got the giggles.

I wasn't stoned. I was buzzed, but this was so wonderful: to see my grandparents laughing. When we walked into KFC they were laughing so hard that all of the Elders there started laughing. They'd never seen my grandparents laugh so hard in their whole lives. Even the cooks came out to look, and they started laughing.

"What's so funny?" my grandfather asked. "Why am I laughing?"

"I don't know," Grandma said. "I'm laughing too!"

I stood there in a garden of laughing Elders. I should have taken pictures or a quick video, but the truth is, I'd just realized what I had done. I'd gotten my beautiful grandparents stoned because of my selfishness and stupidity.

I felt horrible. It was then that I received a bank alert. Money for the whole month had just been deposited in my account, with an apology from the Tłı̨chǫ Government. Somebody thought that this one department had paid me, but I was a new account. I'd fallen between the cracks. I was looking at more money than I had seen in my account in a good long while.

And there we were in KFC with my grandparents wiping their eyes and laughing.

I decided right then and there that I'd quit smoking pot forever.

I also decided to pay for the best weekend of my grandparents' lives.

And it was.

There was KFC, Bingo, Walmart, A&W, The Fat Fox for coffee. My grandfather loved their scones, which he called "baby bannocks," and he loved their coffee. Ehtsı̨ had tea. Black tea with lots of cream. I insisted that they stay at the Super 8, and we did it all over again the next day, with church, shopping and more church before hitting the Independent grocery store and driving back to Behchoko.

As I dropped them off at the Old Folks' Home in Behchoko and helped haul all of their groceries into their suite, I knew they'd be eating well for weeks, if my uncles didn't clean them out first.

After I loaded up their freezer, I felt my grandfather give my shoulder a gentle squeeze.

"Mahsi cho," he said. "Grandson."

I'd never been so proud, and I decided to forgive myself for the marijuana incident.

* * *

My mother found out about the KFC event and called me. She had spoken to my grandparents and then had gone to town on a research mission. My grandparents had left out the American cigarette information, but I suspected my mom suspected. She was the reason I knew in English what everyone at KFC was still talking about.

A few months later, after a bout of pneumonia and a deep cough that he couldn't shake, well, we were all called to spend time with my ehtsèe around his bed. A tough, bossy Tłįchǫ nurse named Jennifer was there from the Health Centre, checking up on both my grandparents. I was scared of her and intrigued at the same time. Jennifer wouldn't make eye contact with me, but she softened whenever she was around Ehtsèe and Ehtsį. It was beautiful to hear them talking Tłįchǫ, and they'd often laugh at inside jokes about things. Sadly, my uncles were still drinking. We could smell it on them. They were already grieving. But I was honoured to be asked to take portraits at what became a family reunion. Cousins, aunts, great-aunts, community. Good food. Lovely hymns. Lots of laughter. Hours of stories, which I recorded with permission, were there for me to start sharing as soon as I returned to my master computer in my little rented home in Behchoko.

My grandfather asked to see my portfolios again. I had ten different albums now that showcased my work. I left to go get them, and when I returned, everyone else had gone home to rest. It was just me, Jennifer and my grandparents. Ehtsèe stirred. He was propped up on many pillows to ease the congestion in his lungs. My grandmother was asleep on the bed, all curled up under a comforter, holding his hand. In her right hand was his pipe. I ache now thinking I should have taken that shot, but I decided to keep it just for myself as a testimony of eternal love.

"Grandson," my ehtsèe called me in a whisper.

I knelt and held his hand. To my surprise, I found myself weeping.

"Grandpa," I whispered. "Ehtsèe."

He started speaking in Tłı̨chǫ, and I started to panic.

Jennifer was in the room making tea.

"What?" I asked. "What is it, Grandpa?"

"Do you want me to translate?" Jennifer asked. It was the first time she had looked at me. She looked directly into my soul.

"Yes, please."

"Do you have any of those John Wayne cigarettes?" he asked me, with Jennifer translating.

I shook my head. "Inle," I said. "Sorry. They stopped making them. Too tough for the people."

"Eschia," he said. "I could sure use one right now."

I nodded. "I know. Maybe just rest. Sleep. Dream."

He looked up at the ceiling, and I wondered if this was it.

He spoke and Jennifer translated. "What do you think happened to that mushroom and that little boy?"

I was worried that if I didn't say something, we'd lose him. I motioned to Jennifer, and she sat down beside me and put her hand on my shoulder.

To this day, I don't know what came over me. I used both of my hands to hold his.

"Ehtsèe, I think what happened was E.T. would come back to Earth time and time again to help that little boy as he grew. Like maybe Elliott had a reading disability? So E.T. used the power of the glow in his dark finger and healed the boy by touching his lymph nodes and his third eye, and then Elliott was a straight-A student after that. No one could figure it out. How had back-of-the-class gone right to the top? It was a miracle. Then Elliott grew up and he met someone very special and decided to get married, but he was worried that E.T. would miss out, so he and his sweetie decided to have a garden wedding with fireworks after, to let E.T. know he was just fine, that he was no longer alone. And when Elliott was saying his vows and looking out at the crowd, really, he was looking for his little buddy made of mushrooms, and to his surprise a whole bunch of E.T.s all started waving at him, and there was his buddy too. Elliott started to cry. Through his tears he could see all of the E.T.s raising their hands, and all of their pointing fingers lit up with radiant love, in salutes just like AC/DC when they sing "For Those About to Rock," but it was for friendship and best wishes. So, Grandpa, my beautiful ehtsèe, I believe with all my heart that is what happened to the mushroom and the little boy who grew up to be a great father and a loving husband and, one day, an ehtsèe like you."

I felt his hand fall away. Jennifer squeezed my shoulder, sending me strength. I looked up through my tears. My grandfather was snoring.

"Geez," she whispered. "I thought that was it."

Thank goodness that he hadn't passed while I was sharing a web of warmed-up fibs.

"Thank you," I said. "Mahsi cho."

She went back to not looking at me. "Are these photo books yours?" she asked.

"Have a look," I said. "Yes."

I went to make tea and could still feel the spirit of her hand on my back.

We had two more days with my ehtsèe, with the entire community praying, with many visitors stopping by. Jennifer translated for me and stayed with us, even during her downtime.

I had a dream that second night: Jennifer was reaching around with one hand in a smoky room for a perfect line of light. She traced the light in the heart of her palm. Then I watched her walk barefoot into the snow with a little

cross fox trailing her. She stopped and held her hand out,
and the little fox came up and pressed its nose into her
palm, where the light warmed it. Jennifer looked back at
me in the dream and smiled.

When Ehtsèe passed, he sighed.

I felt him pass through me as I held his feet and cried.

Grandma cried. My mom cried. We all cried. Even
Jennifer.

I believe that his dog was waiting for him, so happy
to see him again. I believe they made their spirit trails
through the Mackenzie Mountains to be with their families before attending the big feast in the sky.

The night Ehtsèe passed, the power lines outside the
church hummed under the pads of my moccasined feet as
my spirit floated toward the highway.

"Grandson," a voice said, and I looked left. I couldn't
see him, but I felt his presence. "Let's fly," he said.

We soared and flew north together. As we flew, we saw
the trees get smaller and smaller. We saw the mountains.

"Look," he said, and I did. Thousands and thousands of
caribou were waiting. I could see little ones leaping. Year-
lings. It was like an ocean of antlers. They were so strong.

"When you hold your dreaming daughter," he told me,
"you bring her back here. Show her."

I promised that I would.

"Keep honouring the people," he said. "I am so proud
of you."

And with that I realized his voice was going up and up,
and I soared above the caribou. Many of them looked up. I
waved. But I flew to Fort Smith, of all places, when I knew

I should return to my body in Behchoko. I could see Fort Smith's water tower, the church, Kaesers, the Northern, the drugstore. I could see Roaring Rapids Hall, a.k.a. Moccasin Square Gardens.

The next morning, I awoke in my old bed in my loft in our log house. The smell in that house hit me like a brick: drinking. Hard drinking. Sweat. Old booze.

As I climbed down the stairs onto the main floor, I saw bottles everywhere. People had been smoking in our house too. I was so mad it felt like someone was dragging a rusty fork back and forth across my soul.

Patrick's jaw dropped when he saw me. He was cooking for some blonde woman. She was petite. And smoking. No one was allowed to smoke in our house. The woman's hair was cut short. There were hickeys all over her neck.

"Holy shit," he said. The woman stood, tucking my mother's bathrobe tight. "How did you get here?"

I looked around. The house was the same. "I came in late last night," I bluffed. "In town for work."

He looked at his girlfriend, and she looked at me. She pulled the collar of my mom's housecoat up to cover Patrick's hickeys. But it was too late. We had all felt something drop in the room.

The Fort Smither came out in me. I decided not to be phased, to be polite, to bide my time and get to the truth.

"I'm Paula. Pleased to meet you," the woman said, and we shook hands.

I bowed and said the same.

"Want some eggs and toast?" Patrick asked, avoiding my eyes. He was blushing. "I have bacon."

"Sure," I said. I realized I was starving.

"I should go," Paula said. She walked down the hall toward the room my mother had shared with Patrick for years. I looked over at the chair at the head of the table, where my father's favourite shirt had always hung. It was gone. Patrick had promised us he'd always leave it there as a sign of respect. I knew my mom didn't have it.

I went to Patrick and hugged him. He smelled rancid: booze sweat, perfume and vomit. This was a hug of goodbye. This was my father's house. He knew it. I knew it. Patrick had broken us now and forever.

"Want some coffee?" he asked.

"Sure," I said.

He poured, and I took my cup. We sat quietly. The radio playing could never be loud enough to drown out the panic in the room.

"I'm sorry," he said finally, as he raised the coffee to his lips. "I'm sorry you came home to this."

"Me too."

"I'll move out tomorrow," he said.

Underneath the couch, covered in lint and hair, I could see my father's shirt. I pulled it out, dusted it off, put it back where it belonged.

"Okay," I said.

It was then I got a shock. I felt my grandfather's pipe in my pants pocket. A divine gift. I would take out the pipe later, make a fire and drop tobacco into the flames and pray. For now, I stayed sitting at the table we had bought from Kaesers right before my father passed.

Patrick cooked in silence. I let him. Words would only

get in the way. Underneath the table, I folded my hands together. How would I tell my mother what had happened, or should I? Shamans were secretive, I knew. They had to be. I could feel Jennifer's hand on my back, and my palms were already calling our dreaming daughter's name.

Knock Knock

Everyone knows I have a crush on the Crees.

So I designed a little joke to honour them.

In my joke, there are two Kookums sitting together at the four-way stop in Fort Smith, NWT. My hometown.

One Kookum says, "Knock knock."

The other says, "Who's there?"

A truck passes and a little girl calls out, "Aunty!"

Both Kookums wave back.

"Who was that?" one asks.

The other shrugs. "Our niece, I guess."

They both squint to see if they know the truck, but they've missed it.

"Okay, what?"

"What?"

"Mah. You said you had a joke."

"Oh! Well, okay, where was I?"

"You said 'Knock knock.'"

"Wah Stagaatz."

"Stagaatz you," the other one says, waving a mosquito away. "Go before Bingo, you."

"Oh," the first one says. "Okay, so knock knock."

"Who's there?"

"Ooh hoo."

"Ooh hoo who?"

The one leans into the other one and gives her a gentle elbow. "You're an owl, er nah?"

"Mah?" the older one says, turning her hearing aid up.

They look at the ravens on the steeple of the church. The design of the church appeared in a dream to the late Bishop two Bishops ago. They both know that story.

"What?"

"What what?"

"Okay, so, knock knock."

"Who's there?"

"Oh!" the one says. "I thought you were talking about your ex."

"Which one?"

"My ex."

They laugh.

"Oh! I get it," the other one says. "Ooh hoo is an owl."

"Yes!" The first one says. They laugh and laugh, leaning on each other, as everyone drives by smiling.

"What are they laughing about?" one child asks her mom as they watch the Kookums laugh and wave around their Bingo dabbers.

"Those two," says the child's mother. "Always laughing. Like two little plump budgies."

"Knock knock," the child calls from the back seat.

"Who's there?" her dad asks, smiling.

"Boo," the child says.

"Boo hoo," her dad says.

"Oh, so sad," the child says. She puts her hand on his shoulder. "Don't cry, Dad. I'll always be here for you."

The child's mother puts her hand in her husband's and they drive on, smiling.

PS: In case you didn't know, Cousins, Kookum *is grandmother in Cree.*

I Have to Trust

that all the friends and family we've lost along our
    way
are the first to hold the babies who never made it into
    our hands
or left too soon

So that when we see each other at the great feast in
    the sky
our loved ones will hand us our beautiful babies first
    and hold them with us together
to become an even bigger family
and be whole in our hearts and spirits
forever...

AfterWords

Mahsi cho for reading my stories. I am so grateful to you.

Several of these stories appeared elsewhere in superb anthologies before Barbara Pulling and Cheryl Cohen—my editors—and I worked together to hone them for this collection. I am grateful to both Barbara and Cheryl for being such incredible editors. Mahsi cho, Barbara and Cheryl! I am in awe of you both.

"Aliens" was published in *Love Beyond Body, Space, and Time: An Indigenous LGBT Sci-Fi Anthology* (edited by Hope Nicholson; Bedside Press, 2016). This story is for Carla Ulrich and Smokii Sumac and for everyone in Fort Smith.

"Super Indians" appeared in *Impact: Colonialism in Canada* (edited by Warren Cariou, Katherena Vermette and Niigaanwewidam James Sinclair; published by Manitoba First Nations Education Resource Centre, 2017). Dene Cho appears as the main character in my novella *When We Play Our Drums, They Sing!* (published by McKellar

& Martin Publishing Group, 2018). I'd like to dedicate this story to Monique Gray Smith, Tonya Martin, Meghan Hague and Katrina Chappell.

"Wheetago War I: Lying in Bed Together" was published in *CLI-Fi: Canadian Tales of Climate Change* (edited by Bruce Meyer; Exile Editions, 2017). I'd like to dedicate this story to Bryn and Colm Herbert a.k.a. King Doom and King Gloom.

"Wheetago War II: Summoners" was published in the Inhabit Media horror anthology *Taaqtumi*, in 2019. It is dedicated to Amanda Spotted Fawn and Bracken Hanuse.

"The Promise" is dedicated to Jon Liv Jaque, Richard Mercredi Jr., Joel Duthie, Chris Paul, Trevor Cameron, Leif Gregersen, Dusty Kamps, Graeme Comyn, Garth Prosper, Mike Mahussier, James Croizier, Shane Turgeon, Alex Russo and to my brothers Roger, Johnny and Jamie.

"Man Babies" is dedicated to all of the man babies out there. You know who you are ... and so do we. :)

"I Am Filled with a Trembling Light" is dedicated to Rose and Ric Richardson and Gregory Scofield.

"Ehtsèe/Grandpa" is dedicated to the memory of my ehtsèe, Pierre Wah-Shee, and my ehtsı̨, Melanie Wah-shee. I would also like to thank Rosa Mantla, Dr. Leslie Saxon, Terri Naskan, Tony Rabesca, my Uncle Alexis Washie, my mom, Rosa Wah-shee, Barb and Richard Mercredi Sr., Earl and Marlene Evans and Michel Labine and his family and the late Jennifer Naedzo for helping me craft this story.

"Knock Knock" is dedicated to all of our Elders, especially Irene Sanderson, Seraphine Evans, Helena Mandeville, Rosa Mercredi, Marilyn Buffalo, Bob Cardinal, Dora Torangeau and Henry and Eileen Beaver.

"I Have to Trust" is dedicated to my wife, Keavy Martin, and to Ekwo, our spirit daughter.

* * *

I am grateful to the Canadian Consortium on Performance and Politics in the Americas for support with this work. They gave me a laptop when my war pony of a computer crossed over. Mahsi cho!

I am also grateful to the Metro Edmonton Federation of Libraries in Alberta for letting me be their Writer in Residence in 2017.

I am grateful too to Athabasca University for having me as Writer in Residence for 2017–18.

I am grateful. Mahsi cho, everyone. Bless you all. Mahsi!

Richard Van Camp

An internationally renowned storyteller and best-selling author, Richard Van Camp was born in Fort Smith, Northwest Territories, and is a member of the Tłįchǫ Dene Nation. He acted as a cultural consultant for CBC Television's *North of 60*. A graduate of the En'owkin School of Writing in Penticton, he completed his Bachelor of Fine Arts in Writing at the University of Victoria and completed his Master's of Creative Writing at the University of British Columbia. Richard was awarded Storyteller of the Year for both Canada and the US by the Wordcraft Circle of Native Writers and Storytellers. He is the author of twenty-two books including the novel *The Lesser Blessed* (Douglas & McIntyre, 1996).